Betrayed

DELTA FAMILY ROMANCES #4

CAMI CHECKETTS

Birch River
PUBLISHING

Copyright

Free Book

Receive a free copy of *Seeking Mr. Debonair: The Jane Austen Pact* by clicking here and signing up for Cami's newsletter.

Chapter One

Emery Reeder walked along the Hafen Lake Park Trail in Mesquite, Nevada. Her headlamp cast eerie shadows from the bushes and trees to the lake's calm surface. It was June, four-thirty in the morning, and already eighty degrees. Sheesh. She didn't reside in Hades, but summer in Mesquite was a close neighbor.

As soon as the sun came up, being outside was like being the chocolate chip cookie dough on the top shelf of an oven. In her humble opinion, cookie dough was ruined by cooking it and should always be consumed raw. She figured she shouldn't let herself be cooked, either.

Sleep was overrated and baking from the outside in wasn't good, but fresh air was a necessity. So Emery stubbornly set an alarm for four a.m., placed said alarm across the room, and then crawled on hands and knees to the alarm as it screeched through the formerly peaceful room each morning. It was only way to force herself outside before sane people woke for the day.

She'd agreed to help teach summer school this year, excited about the extra money and extra time with some of the students who struggled, forgetting the misery of staying in Mesquite throughout the summer. Not that she had anywhere exciting to go. She adored teaching fourth grade and thought her little people were hilarious. If she could keep the parents from the extremes of either indifference about their children's futures or trying to bulldoze their children's paths, she'd have no complaints about her job.

In the four years since she'd graduated college, Emery had been completely self-sufficient. She'd had to rely on scholarships, grants, and early morning janitorial work to make it through college, and she was grateful to be past that. She was an independent woman, and she needed to stand on her own two feet.

Over the past four years she'd saved like Ebenezer Scrooge, living on eggs, no-name peanut butter, and all the fruits and veggies she could harvest from hours spent in her church's community garden after work. It had been worth it. She'd saved enough for a large down-payment on her cottage. She'd dubbed her little home "the Shack," and she loved having a place that was *hers*.

Now she could eat meat occasionally, but she was still building her savings account back up. Hence the desperate move of teaching summer school instead of renting a cabin in the woods or flying to visit a college friend. Maybe she would soldier through the drive to Salmon, Idaho to visit her favorite foster family. Or hitchhike, the price of gas being the obscenity it was. Was hitchhiking even legal? She could ride her beach cruiser. That wouldn't get old for seven hundred miles. She could imagine her aching rear end already. Could she earn an iron butt award or something cool like that, or was that just for Harley guys? She wasn't riding seven hundred miles in leather chaps. The award wasn't worth that.

Her phone rang, startling her from her random thoughts. She yanked it out and stared at the unknown number. Chicago area code. Her brother was stationed at Great Lakes Naval Base in Chicago, but he hadn't called often since she'd seen him six months ago after he returned from Iraq. They used to be so close, and she never expected that the distance his deployment put between them might never be healed.

His last deployment had irrevocably changed him. They still talked over FaceTime occasionally and texted often, but he wasn't himself. She kept praying he could be healed, maybe find a sweetheart of a woman to mend his heart. As a civilian, she had no idea what Travis had gone through as an Ensign in the Navy during two deployments. She used to ask him to share, but he always told her she was too good to be exposed to what he'd seen and done.

Had he gotten a new number? Then her chest tightened as panic hit her full force. What if it was someone calling on his behalf and something was horribly wrong?

She slid the phone on. "Travis?"

"Miss Reeder?" a compassionate male voice asked

"Yes?"

"I regret to be the one to inform you that your brother was killed in a special ops mission."

Emery's stomach filled with acid. Her vision swam and she stopped walking as her legs turned to lead. She clung to the phone as her worst nightmare became reality.

Dead? Travis? There wasn't a bench nearby, so she sank onto the trail cross-legged and leaned her head into her hand. Horror washed over her and cold sweat covered her body.

She prayed desperately for it to not be true. How could her brother be dead?

Yet hadn't she always known his military path was dangerous? She'd dreaded something like this happening, had tried to prepare herself. Her stomach churned, and she swallowed down bile. There was no possible way to prepare for something like this.

How had he been killed? Where? When? Travis had never told her he was special ops. She swallowed and tried to speak, but she had so many questions and no idea where to start. Travis had told her how closed-mouth the military was. She doubted this man would tell her the details of his death. Did she even want to know? It would make it too sickeningly real.

"Miss Reeder? I can't imagine how troubling this is. Are you all right?"

Not all right. She couldn't even speak it hurt so bad.

"Are you there, ma'am?"

She cleared her throat. "I'm here," she managed. There were no tears. They'd come. Soon. She didn't even know how to mourn losing her only family member. Crumple into a ball and never move again?

She and Travis had been inseparable as children, shuffled through foster care homes when their mom was declared unfit and forced to give up her rights. Travis had been five and Emery three. She didn't even remember her mom and nobody knew who their dads were besides knowing they weren't the same person, as Travis had obvious Hispanic heritage.

Their foster parents through high school, the Weatherspoons, were good, solid Christians. They'd never been able to have children and weren't always patient with two rambunctious teenagers as fifty-year-old first-time parents, but they'd done their best. Emery still drove the ten hours to Salmon once or twice a year to visit them and talked to them on holidays and birthdays.

Travis had joined the military at eighteen with the help of Sister Weatherspoon, as her foster mom had insisted they call her, and he'd flourished. When Emery graduated high school two years later, she'd applied for every scholarship and grant she could find online and had been awarded quite a few of them. After she made it through Boise State University with an elementary education degree, she'd found the job at Virgin Valley Elementary School. She'd thought she was ready for year-round warmth, but had been a little naïve about how miserable the heat could be.

She and Travis had grown apart because of the physical distance between them, but they'd been fiercely loyal to each other as only two orphaned siblings could be. They emailed, texted, called, and got together any chance they had. Until his last deployment.

She loved her brother and said a desperate prayer that he would be welcomed by his Savior on the other side.

"H-how did he die?" she croaked out.

"I'll tell you what I know, which I'm sorry to say is more than you'll hear from the Navy. They are not acknowledging his death as honorable, and you will receive no compensation or sympathy from the U.S. Government."

"What? Why?" That was horrible.

"His mission was so deep that it couldn't be sanctioned. If I'm correct, they will even list him as AWOL from his company."

Every word was a hit to the gut. Even if she'd lost the closeness to her brother more recently, he'd been her constant, her protector, and her buddy growing up. He was the only family she had.

Dead. Disgraced. Not acknowledged.

"Where's his body?" she asked. "A funeral?"

"You'll be contacted soon about his death and they'll ask you what you want to do for his funeral. They'll get his body to you, but that's about all they'll do for you." His voice wasn't as compassionate now, more bitter.

"Who are you?"

"Someone who knew and respected your brother. Who saw how good and loyal he was, willing to risk his life and give everything for the country he loved."

Emery teared up then. It was true. Travis was a patriot through and through.

"Sadly, those he was willing to bleed and die for turned their backs on your brother. They have hidden or more likely destroyed all evidence of the mission that Ensign Reeder sacrificed himself for. He isn't the first soldier to be treated so poorly by the country he loved. His memory, and everything he stood for, will be regarded as a disgrace. Is that what you want for your brother?"

"No," she croaked out. Ah, Travis. He had given his life for his country, but nobody would ever know.

"I didn't think so."

"But who are you?" she asked again. She'd assumed he was with the military, but maybe not with the way he was talking about the Navy.

"I can't reveal that, Miss Reeder, without placing myself, but more importantly you, in danger. We both know Ensign Reeder would want me to help you and watch out for you."

That warmed her heart. Travis was trying to watch out for her, even from the other side.

"I can tell you I am someone who worked closely with Ensign Reeder. I am someone who can help you find answers and hopefully peace."

She sucked in a breath. She was confused, weak, and nauseated. All she wanted was to be alone and just sob, but she had to ask, not knowing if this man could even tell her the truth, "Who killed him?"

"A man named Greer Delta." The man's voice was so crisp and detached, like he was a robot. "A civilian with top level battle training. He masquerades as a quiet rancher, but is actually a lethal weapon."

Greer Delta. It was an odd name. A mean name. Greer Delta. A gangster maybe? Greer. Growl, snarl, howl, roar, bark, or yap. She and her students loved to tease and list synonyms. She'd stick with growl. His name growled at her. Why had that awful man killed her brother?

"Why did he kill Travis? What kind of mission was Travis on?"

6

"He was tasked with obtaining a secret weapon that nobody but Greer Delta and his family know the location or existence of."

"You know it," she pointed out. "Travis knew it."

"I know ... about it. Travis was close to finding answers that would have blessed his military brothers and sisters with a weapon that would save countless American lives." His voice was suddenly bitter. There had to be a story there, but Emery couldn't find it in her to dig it out. This guy's issues weren't something she could solve. She couldn't even solve her own. "I assumed your highly competent brother and his teammates could find it for me. They were foiled by the ones protecting and hiding the weapon."

That hurt. Not as bad as his death, but that Travis had sacrificed his life for a failed mission was so empty and tragic. She hated it.

"You alone can redeem your brother and finish his mission. Only you Emery can make his sacrifice worth it."

"Pardon me?" Redeeming her brother sounded good, but if Travis couldn't accomplish some mission, she'd have no chance at it. Travis was strong, trained, competent, and a leader. Emery was a chatterbox softie who didn't even know how to hold a pistol. "I'm no soldier. I'm a schoolteacher."

"I know exactly who and what you are. This is a case where a civilian will uncover more information and leads than professional soldiers. You can do an incredible service for your country, all while honoring your brother's memory."

Sheesh. No pressure. She didn't even know who this guy was. What if he was some psycho who'd sent Travis on this impossible mission? What if he *was* responsible for her brother's death? Actually, he was if he had put her brother in proximity to the evil Greer Delta. The growling murderer. Evil, malevolent, criminal, malicious, wicked.

She tried to focus. Was this man asking her to redeem her brother's death for the military and the United States, or did he have his own agenda?

"If you know exactly who I am, then you know I'm an expert borderline skilled connoisseur of grammar, synonyms, and arts and crafts, but I loathe algebra. So my special set of skills is going to somehow *make this right* and avenge my brother's death?" She didn't mean to be sarcastic, but there was no way she could go on some special ops mission.

"With your innocent beauty, you are the perfect candidate to play on the chauvinistic sympathies of the reclusive Greer Delta, work your way into his life, become a guest in his home, and find the secret. As soon as you obtain the location, you will send me the details and you can bug out with my blessing. I will then assign a special ops team to finish the mission. Your country and your brother will be forever grateful to you." The man had completely ignored her sarcasm and heaped on more guilt and crazy ideas.

"Uh, come again?" Icy fear traced through her, causing her to shiver even in the morning heat. "You expect me to get chummy with the man who murdered my brother?"

"Our intel suggests you would be in absolutely no danger."

"Oh, thank you. I feel so reassured now." This guy was a little off. He'd seemed compassionate and loyal to Travis, but he was willing to put her in a dangerous situation because of her "innocent beauty." She'd give him innocent beauty. This dude had put her brother in a mortally dangerous situation, and now he wanted to do the same to her. These Deltas sounded like bad news. She wouldn't mind writing an impeccably composed but downright nasty hate mail letter to Greer Delta, filled with lots of deplorable synonyms about his murderous heart, but she didn't want to go anywhere near him.

"The Delta family are upright Christian people who respect and protect women. Greer Delta would never dream of hurting you. I swear that to you on your brother's honor."

He was laying it on thick. "Forgive me for doubting you, but the *saintly* man who murdered my brother is a Christian who respects and protects women?" She was so confused. She hated Greer Delta, was reeling from the loss of Travis, and had no idea why this guy thought she was the solution to their military's and country's problems with some hidden weapon. She shuddered. Was this a nuclear weapon and the evil Deltas were going to take the entire country out if she didn't stop them? That was far too much pressure for an untrained schoolteacher, and she needed to stop watching action movies recommended by her students.

"Yes. He and his family have been deluded into believing they are protecting the weapon for the good guys." He gave a harsh laugh at that. "Deluded, misguided, false patriots, the whole bunch of them."

"This is all ... psychotic," Emery admitted. So the Deltas weren't Satan's henchmen but a bunch of zealots killing her brother because they'd been tricked by the sneaky bad guys? It was more than psychotic.

"I'm sure it seems that way. I apologize for throwing so much at you after you just learned of your brother's loss, but we need you. I need you. Your country needs you. Travis needs you."

His words touched something deep inside her. She loved her and she loved her country, just like Travis had. She'd always felt her way to help others was to be the best teacher she could and love, inspire, and lift her students. The problem was she had no concept of military strategy and fighting. Even if she wouldn't be in danger confronting the evil Greer Delta, anger and resentment would eat her up if she had to come face to face with the man.

"I think it's a better route for me to mourn my brother, not avenge him," she said finally. She tried to be a saint herself. No way was Greer Delta one. *Vengeance is mine*, it said somewhere in the scriptures. She had to leave all this pain to God or she'd become a bitter, withered harpy. Though admittedly vengeance sounded pretty appetizing right now, she was realistic enough to know that if her well-trained brother couldn't best this Greer Delta, no way would she stand a chance.

"If you are willing to let your brother's legacy fade to nothing, and never get the answers about why he had to die, you can choose that selfish route."

Ouch. This guy seemed compassionate, but he didn't pull punches.

"Are you even going to tell me who you are?" She wasn't committing to anything right now. She needed to figure out a funeral and cry a lot and call the Weatherspoons and let them know what had happened. Was there anybody else who would want to know about Travis's passing? He hadn't run with the best crowd in high school and most of them were drugged out, in prison, or busy fathering children across the state of Idaho. She didn't know his military friends. *Please say he had good friends*, she begged heaven above.

A heaviness settled on her heart. Travis's death was tragic for so many reasons. He'd had so much unfulfilled potential. She wished for the millionth time that he hadn't chosen the military route. But that was selfish of her. The military had helped him stay out of prison, away from drugs and irresponsible fatherhood, but it had still killed him in the end. He'd changed and distanced himself from her because of what he'd seen and done in his last deployment. Ultimately he'd sacrificed himself for his country. At least she had that. But if this guy was telling the truth, nobody else believed that. Travis's martyrdom would mean nothing if Emery didn't go put herself on the altar as well. Her only qualifications were her innocent beauty and the need to avenge her brother. It wasn't enough.

"I wish I could tell you more," the voice said, "but that would only put you at risk."

"And somehow weaseling my way into my brother's murderer's house isn't putting me at risk?"

"I promise you on my son's grave that you will be in no danger from Greer Delta or any of the Delta family."

"I'm sorry about your son," she managed. Was that why his voice had seemed almost tortured and bitter at times?

The man didn't respond to that. "Your country needs you, Miss Delta. Will you do this small favor for them? For Travis?"

She couldn't confirm that yet. Small favor? It seemed massive, huge, colossal, immense to her. "I don't know."

The man didn't seem fazed. "The details of your assignment are in your mailbox, along with two hundred thousand dollars in cash and a fake ID."

"Yikes! What am I going to do with two hundred thousand dollars?" Actually, she could think of a lot she could do with that kind of money, but not if she hadn't earned it. The fact that he knew where she lived and had been to her house was disturbing too. He seemed like the good guy, but what did she know?

"You can use it for funeral expenses, travel expenses, and whatever else you need for your assignment, and then keep any surplus with your country's thanks."

She didn't want the money, but funeral expenses? She hadn't even thought of that.

"The question is, Miss Delta... Will you avenge your brother's death, finish what he gave his life for, save America from imminent destruction, and find answers that no one else can give you?"

"That's a loaded question."

"I don't know that you'll ever have to answer a more important one."

Emery had no clue how to respond. She'd landed in the middle of a spy novel. She would have to pray hard for guidance on which path to take. If she didn't feel she should complete her brother's assignment, she didn't care what this guy said. She'd get his money back to him and pray he'd leave her alone.

"I'll check back soon." The man hung up.

She dropped her phone and buried her head in her hands.

Curse Greer Delta. Curse, jinx, plague, afflict, scourge, torment that man. She didn't want to avenge her brother or rescue her country. All she wanted was her brother back.

Chapter Two

Greer Delta finished feeding and watering his horses and then walked out of his barn into the summer evening. It was the first of July and absolutely beautiful in his family's remote, lush mountain valley. He wandered over to the fence where his steers were grazing. The fence line stretched up into the trees and then a mile to the south end of the valley until it connected with the lake as the eastern boundary.

He'd built his house, barn, and corrals half a mile around the lake, distancing himself from the rest of his family. He loved his family. They were great people, and they had his back. But he craved privacy and needed quiet. They'd all been respectful of that.

Killing a man last week had changed everything. Since then, he'd had this unfamiliar urge for human company and contact. Which made no sense to him and would've confused everyone who knew him ... if he'd been willing to open his mouth and talk to anybody about it.

His mom claimed that even as a child, he'd been sober and would arch away from anyone wanting to hold him close. Probably a character flaw. He didn't know, but he wasn't one to waste time stewing about his silence or anybody's interpretation of it. He worked hard on his ranch, raising the best beef cattle in Colorado, and trained diligently as part of the Delta Protection Detail to protect a secret that he didn't even have the privilege of knowing. He didn't ask questions or seek anyone's attention. Except for his former girlfriend Belinda, the other women he'd kissed had initiated the dating and the kissing. He'd liked it. A lot. But he'd never found a woman besides Belinda that he craved talking to enough to give up his peaceful, contented life. He read a lot of books—crime fiction and religious nonfiction—and if he got bored, he turned on a country song.

But he wasn't contented anymore, and no book or country song could distract him from the anguish. In his dreams and during the day, he could still see it. He, Uncle Joseph, and his cousin Colt had searched together for a day and a half, not sleeping and barely eating or drinking. Papa, his dad, and Thor had searched other areas in the mountains, along with Sheriff Reed and some trusted friends from town.

He, Uncle Joseph, and Colt had finally heard gunshots and found the men who'd kidnapped Klein and Alivia decimating an old cabin in the woods. His Uncle Joseph had shot and killed one man out front while Greer and his cousin Colt had tackled the other one. Colt had pinned the guy down and told Greer to find Alivia. With the two aggressors subdued, Greer had rushed toward the blown-out windows of the little cabin, yanking his pistol from his hip holster as he ran. He prayed his cousin Alivia and her business partner Klein were still alive, and wondered where Travis Reeder had disappeared to.

He'd found all three of them. The mercenary and kidnapper had been framed in the back door of the cabin, pointing a gun at Klein and Alivia and saying, "It's time to die." Like some James Bond movie.

Greer passed a hand over his face, no longer seeing the peaceful green meadow bordered by the lake, the thick trees, the picturesque mountain, and the blue summer sky.

Instinct born of years and years of training by his grandpa, an elite military man, had taken over. He'd fired before Travis Reeder could kill Klein or Alivia. He'd shot Reeder straight through the head just as he'd done in target practice thousands of times. Everybody had proclaimed him a hero.

He was no hero. He'd simply reacted to protect his cousin and his friend. Everyone assumed he was being humble about saving their lives, not taking credit because Greer never wanted anyone to fuss over him. But the truth was, it was a horrific weight to have taken a man's life. Even if the man was a mercenary, a deserter hired to steal the Delta secret, had resorted to kidnapping to do it, and been willing to kill for a huge paycheck.

Papa seemed to be the only one who understood Greer's anguish and struggle. His grandfather had spent years in the military. Greer had never asked how many men he'd had to kill, but he knew it had happened. Papa had come over twice in the past week, brought take-out, and watched a couple of Chandler's lacrosse games with Greer. Chandler was a huge success in the PLL and they were all very proud.

Last night, Papa had showed him the footage of Travis Reeder's graveside service. It was held at a pretty cemetery in Salmon, Idaho. There had only been four people at the ten-minute long service: the preacher, an older couple Papa explained were Reeder's foster parents throughout high school, and a sister.

Emery Reeder. She'd been much, much prettier than the beautiful setting. Long dark curly hair, deep-brown eyes, and an angelic-looking face.

It had ripped him apart to see the silent tears tracing down her face as she buried her brother. Did she have any clue how or why he'd died? It wasn't a service with military honors, so she must've at least known he'd gone AWOL. Compassion swelled in him.

Why Papa had felt Greer needed to watch the service he couldn't say; maybe just to help him feel compassion for this woman.

He sat through it without a word. Not that Greer ever said much. Then he'd listened as Papa told him Miss Reeder was a school-teacher in Nevada, no criminal history, loved by her students and their parents, and appeared to be an upstanding citizen. She and Travis had been shuffled through foster care, and she'd put herself through Boise State University while Travis had joined the military. Who knew why Travis had gone AWOL and become a mercenary, but the military life was hard on a lot of men.

His sister looked to be doing good things. And Greer was responsible for leaving her without family. Here he was surrounded by a loving family, but he'd taken Emery Reeder's only brother.

Papa focused the power of his penetrating blue gaze on him and said, "I know what you're going through. I've been there. All the reassurances that you had no choice but to take that shot—that Reeder would've killed Klein or Alivia if you hadn't—won't help. I have to ask one thing, though. If you hadn't reacted instinctively and taken that shot and Alivia or Klein were dead, would you have been able to live with yourself any better?"

Greer's eyes widened. "No," he admitted. Of course he would've chosen to protect Alivia and Klein. The fact remained that Reeder had kidnapped them so he could discover the Delta family secret for a fat paycheck and had been about to kill one of them because it hadn't gone according to plan and he was furious about it. Reeder had likely been unreasonable and out of his head because Alivia and Klein had escaped.

"I didn't think so." Papa took a breath. "You've taken a life, Greer. It's one of the hardest things to reconcile in your mind and heart because life is precious and we've been commanded not to kill. Throughout the scriptures, there are many, many examples of times God's people had to kill. Killing Travis Reeder wasn't optional and

I'm so grateful you didn't hesitate, that you fired instinctively and protected Alivia and Klein. But I also can't tell you what it means to me that you're not taking the responsibility lightly. The very fact that I can see the torture in your eyes tells me your heart is soft and you would never hurt someone needlessly."

Greer's heart slammed against his ribs. Papa understood. Of course he did.

"Will it stop hurting?" he asked.

"In time, and with prayer."

Greer needed to pray, but he'd felt too stirred up. He pointed at the computer they'd watched the graveside service on. "How do I help?"

"I don't know that you can help Emery Reeder, but you can pray for her."

Greer nodded slowly. Maybe he didn't know what to pray that would help him or her, but he could at least pray for her to feel God's peace and sustaining power.

"God will help her." Papa's gaze grew even more intense. "And He will help you. Only your Savior can take away the pain. Turn to Him, Greer. Always turn to Him."

That hit him hard. Papa was right. Greer wanted to move past the pain and find peace.

So he'd spent hours last night while he should've been sleeping praying for Emery Reeder to be surrounded and lifted by hosts of angels and praying the good Lord could make things right for that lady and that she could find peace and comfort.

Now he stared at the cows munching on grass and realized the sun was setting. Dang, he was good at wasting time lately. No one blamed him and everyone was understanding and supportive, but he wanted to somehow move past this.

The Delta Protection Detail had been escalating lately and sadly, he needed to be ready to fight and protect and possibly to kill again.

One of his siblings or cousins would be chosen to be the secret keeper by Papa. Greer would accept the responsibility if needed, but he thought his older sister Alivia was the best choice. She was brilliant, steady, calm, had helped raise him and his crazy brothers proving how unruffled she could be, and she had military training in addition to Delta family training. He'd have to wait and see how that played out.

Papa feared his close friend General Seamons was leaking information about the secret, but he had no proof of that. The only surviving kidnapper, Colby Newman, had sworn up and down that he had no idea who'd hired them, and Travis had been the only one to communicate with the man. Colby didn't think Travis even knew who the man was. He admitted he thought Flynn did, but of course Flynn was dead, so that was no help.

The only good news was whoever had backed the kidnapping and was trying to get to the Delta secret hadn't appeared to share it with anyone else. They didn't have droves of people showing up to find the "treasure." For the past week they'd upped surveillance, but all had been quiet. He could be grateful for that.

Greer bowed his head and said another prayer before heading in for the night. He prayed once more—it seemed to be his all-consuming pastime lately—the secret would stay safe, his family would be protected, and Emery Reeder would find peace and happiness.

The snap of a branch in the nearby forest brought his head up before he could say amen. He searched around and quickly pinpointed a flash of pink in the trees. Pink? That wasn't a natural color in the woods by any means.

He slid his Smith and Wesson .500 pistol out of the holster on his hip and cautiously crept forward. His reaction told him he'd shoot again if needed. Was that a horrible character defect, or just instinctive training? He would download some books on psychology, mili-

18

tary, and intuitive protectiveness tonight, but he couldn't worry about it right now. There was definitely an intruder moving through the woods toward him. He should inform Papa, but he could only see and hear one person's movements. If needed, he could pull in the family to help after he checked it out.

He reached the edge of the woods and peered in. The shape moved around a pine tree and came into full view. She saw him and stopped in her tracks. Her eyes went wide and her body visibly trembled.

His breath caught in his chest. A woman. An absolutely gorgeous woman with long brown curls, a smooth, angelic-looking face, deep-brown eyes, and full lips. Her pink T-shirt was snagged and dirty and her gray shorts looked to be the same. Her arms, legs, and even her neck had red scratches and dirt smudges on them.

From running through the woods, or had a person done that to her? If anyone hurt her, he would make them regret it. He didn't want to kill again, but he was all over pummeling some loser who would hurt an innocent woman.

As they stared at each other, a tingling yet peaceful feeling told him this woman was very important and he should help her. He also realized he somehow knew her. How? She definitely wasn't from Summit Valley and Greer didn't get out much.

Her gaze darted from his face, across his upper body, and stopped on the gun in his hand. She gasped and backed up, putting her hand over her mouth and running into the branches of a pine tree.

Greer quickly slid the gun back into its holster and held up both hands. "I won't hurt you."

She pulled in quick breaths, her chest rising and falling so quick he hoped she wouldn't hyperventilate. At least she didn't turn around and run, but she looked far from reassured. Did he scare her?

Suddenly it hit him who this beautiful, disheveled woman was. Emery Reeder. That wasn't possible. Was it? He blinked and studied her again. It was her. He could swear it was. The sister of the man he'd killed. What was she doing here? Did she know who Greer was? That might explain the fear in those brown eyes.

She might look angelic, but the only reason Emery Reeder would walk onto his property was to get revenge for her brother's death or to get the secret Travis had failed to obtain.

How would she know Greer had killed Travis? Only the sheriff and Greer's own family knew that. Right? Was their leak worse than Papa feared?

As they studied each other, all these thoughts and worries stewed, but Greer couldn't disregard the feeling he'd had seconds earlier that she was important and he had to help her. It was insane but he felt like his prayers for her had somehow brought her here. He wanted to stride to her, pull her into his chest, tell her he was sorry, pray with her, and hold her until they healed together.

Of course, he'd never do something that bold. He wouldn't react like that with someone he knew well who'd lost a family member. No way was he going to hold and pray with the woman whose brother he'd killed but somehow he needed to understand why heaven was telling him to protect and be there for her.

He stood there, staring at her. She stared right back. Studied him deeply, as if trying to ascertain if he would murder her too. She looked terrified that he would attack her. If she was scared of him, why would she come here? Was she lost and the angels above had somehow directed her to him? That made about as much sense as anything tonight.

If she knew who he was, of course she'd be terrified. She'd hate him. Greer wouldn't blame her, but he wished he could explain he'd reacted instinctively and he couldn't have allowed Alivia or Klein to die. If only he could've placed the shot anywhere besides Travis Reeder's head. Yet if he had, maybe the man would've gotten his own shot off.

20

The shadows deepened around them, and she didn't seem prone to move or say anything. Greer never was the one to break the silence, but for some reason he felt compelled to. He found it was his responsibility to ask, "Are you in danger?"

Her dark eyes flashed at him and for the first time in his life Greer wondered if *he* was in danger. He couldn't find a reason she would come here, unless it was with evil intent. She couldn't possibly know he'd killed Travis, yet somehow he thought she did.

"Yes," she squeaked out. She looked over her shoulder as if someone was following her. Greer almost pulled his pistol out again, but he didn't want that fear returning to her eyes.

Suddenly, she dodged around some undergrowth and ran at him. Greer stood his ground and braced himself. If Emery Reeder knew who he was and what he'd done, he fully expected her to either stick a knife in his gut or punch him. If she didn't know who he was and truly was in danger, he suddenly imagined her throwing herself into his arms.

He idiotically prayed hard for the latter. Even though he knew that would never be a reality for him and this very surprising woman.

She stopped short of touching him. Dang. Instead, she gazed up into his eyes and whispered, "My boyfriend—well, *ex*-boyfriend. He tried to ..." She swallowed and didn't finish.

His gut churned. He'd dismantle any man who tried to hurt her. Hadn't she been through enough? Raised in foster care and then losing all the family she had—at Greer's hands. But from the way she was looking at him right now, he wasn't certain she had any idea who he was.

It was insane that she would end up in his family's valley. Not just in their valley, but walking right out of the trees and onto Greer's property like an angel from heaven. Had heaven above orchestrated this meeting so Greer could pay penance for killing her brother? He'd have to think about that later. First things first.

He looked over her shoulder, playing along with the ex-boyfriend story, though he imagined there was a ninety-eight percent chance it was a cover for her coming here to avenge her brother's murder and find the secret. "Is he following you?"

"I don't think so." She shuddered and wrapped her arms around herself. "He brought me to the mountains earlier this afternoon. He told me he just wanted to talk and catch up, but then he tried to force himself on me. I got away. I've been running through the mountains for ... hours."

Greer's eyebrows lifted. Running through the mountains for hours would explain why she looked so disheveled. It was far too obvious she'd made up the story about the ex, but she probably had hiked through the mountains so she could arrive at Greer's looking disheveled and in need and play on his sympathies. Had someone helped her with this ploy, or was she acting on her own? How soon until she tried to plunge a knife through his heart?

He hated all these sadistic thoughts and wanted to have faith that the angels were in charge not the devil who'd sent Travis and his buddies after the secret. There was something innocent and pure about Emery Reeder, and he found himself hoping she didn't know who Greer was and he could somehow help her.

"I don't dare go home. He's unstable and dangerous. When I ran, he yelled after me that when he finds me, he'll kill me."

Greer flinched. What if her story was true? How was he supposed to decipher fact or fiction? Greer wasn't proficient at interpersonal communication. He didn't even talk to his animals. "He didn't chase you?"

If there even was a man and the guy wanted to kill her, why would he just stand there and let her go? To toy with her? Greer's gaze darted around on the sheer hope her story would be validated, but he didn't hear or see anything out of the ordinary.

"He ripped his ACL last month playing basketball and luckily he didn't have his gun on him." She shuddered and looked from the gun on Greer's hip, then back to his face.

"We should get you to the police," he said. He'd let his buddy Sheriff Reed get to the bottom of the story and why Emery Reeder had appeared like this. Even as he said and thought that, he found he didn't want her to exit his life as quickly as she'd come into it. He wanted to help her. Especially if heavenly intervention may have brought her here.

"Please no. Justin is a policeman."

His eyes widened. She'd put some decent thought into her story. Unless, by some miracle, she was genuine. "With who?"

"DPD."

Greer swallowed. The Denver Police Department was a lot bigger than Summit Valley's Sheriff's Department and his friend Sheriff Reed. Emery surely knew that. Greer wasn't afraid of anyone, and with his family to back him up could take on an army, but he didn't want to force her to file a statement until she was comfortable. Oh boy. He was tempted to swallow this story lock, stock, and barrel. Maybe if he had more experience with beautiful women, he'd know if she was genuine.

"Please." She looked up at him and he was struck by her beauty and the sweetness in her dark gaze. "Will you protect me?"

"Yes." He nodded solemnly. He'd do anything to make recompense for what he'd done to her. There had to be some kind of heavenly intervention happening here. He'd been praying for her. He'd seen her come out of the woods. Emery Reeder finding him like this when she was possibly in danger had to be a sign from above. Every instinct in him was firing to protect this lady from any more harm.

But there were also a lot of voices in his head shouting that it was all a lie.

"I don't have anybody who can help me." She bit at her full lip. "I grew up in foster care."

Well, at least that felt like the truth.

"Sorry to just show up here and ask for your help." She looked out at the lake for a moment and said, "I have a good feeling around you. Very different from Justin."

She couldn't possibly have a good feeling around him, and she hadn't met his eyes when she'd said that. Yet there was an opportunity here to at least figure out why she'd come and what her agenda was. If she was after the secret like her brother, Greer was duty bound to keep her from finding it. This might be the opportunity his family needed to figure out who had hired her brother and the other men from the Navy.

He studied her. Would she balk if he asked her to stay with him? It was crazy. He prayed briefly, and he still felt like it was a good idea. He had plenty of room. This could be his chance to figure out what she was about and who had hired her brother. It had to be the same person who had sent her after Greer.

If by some miracle she wasn't Emery Reeder, he'd think heaven had sent a gift, an angel for him to protect and get to know.

Emery Reeder. It was surreal that she was standing right in front of him. He'd been praying for some way to help her the moment he'd heard her in the woods. Was this his answer? Greer was supposed to watch over her and somehow help with her grief? That seemed a bit twisted as he'd caused that grief.

"You could stay with me," he said finally.

Her eyes widened, and she twisted her hands together. Her gaze focused in on him and he felt like she could see into his soul. This woman was a Christian, and she was insightful. He could see both. Why would she lie to him like this?

"You'll keep me safe?" she asked softly, and he knew she meant safe in many ways—from the made-up ex, from Greer hurting her, and possibly from whoever had sent her here. She didn't trust Greer, that was obvious, but maybe she would someday and maybe she

24

didn't trust whoever had given her the information and sent her here either. Emery could be a pawn with no one to turn to.

"Yes." He said the word like an oath. He'd keep her safe. But he'd also get a hold of Papa and inform him what was happening. And he'd sleep with his door locked and one eye open.

"Thank you." The words rushed out of her and he'd never loved someone's gratitude so much. "I've been so scared. So alone. You look like a tough, honorable cowboy who will protect me from Justin and anyone else."

Greer didn't know that he'd ever blushed in his life, but he could feel his cheeks heating. He nodded, having no clue what to say to that. He was confused, and she was sticking with her made-up story like glue.

"What's your name?" she asked softly.

He swallowed. Ah. This was a possibility he hadn't explored and explained a lot. She had no idea who she'd run to. Maybe there really was a dangerous ex, though she had lied about being from Denver. Once she found out who he was, she might turn and run back to the ex-boyfriend.

"Greer Delta," he said, his gaze not straying from hers.

She didn't even flinch. So the other possibility surfaced. She had no idea who Greer was or who had killed her brother. It made sense. The military or police department wouldn't have released the details. That led him back to thinking her story might be true.

Yet somehow he felt like she knew who he was, and the story was all fabricated. If she did know who he was, she was an extremely impressive actress and weaseling her way into his life to avenge Travis. He'd played right into that by offering her a stay at his house. He thought it was still smart, though, to keep her close and find out who was really behind all this. No way this innocent beauty would try to infiltrate the Deltas and find the secret on her own.

"What's your name?" he asked. He might have to play a part as well until he figured out why she'd really come and if there even was an ex-boyfriend she was running from.

"Taylor Miles."

Greer flinched. A lie. That meant she knew exactly who he was, and she was going to set him up.

He guessed there could be another option. Maybe she truly wasn't Emery Reeder. Didn't they claim everybody had a twin out there? She and her brother had obviously had different fathers. If she'd had a promiscuous mother, Emery might literally have a twin or sister somewhere in the world who had gotten separated from them in the foster care system. This could be that woman or a woman who looked uncannily like the real Emery Reeder.

He really liked this last theory. She really was Taylor Miles. She was running from her ex-boyfriend. Greer had just been given a gift from heaven.

Sadly, he doubted the easy story was the real one. He had no idea what was truth and what was fiction at this point. All Greer knew was his orderly world was about to get turned upside down.

Chapter Three

Emery's heart was beating so high and fast she could hardly catch a breath. She was standing in front of her brother's murderer and lying to him like a fraud, imposter, hypocrite, perjurer to boot. When she'd first seen him with his gun drawn, looking like a dangerous wild west cowboy outlaw, she'd been sure her life was over. Then he'd stunned her. He'd immediately put his gun away and changed everything about his threatening stance, promising he wouldn't hurt her. She'd never looked into eyes that blue and that sincere. Could she trust he would keep her safe? From himself or whoever had ordered him to kill her brother?

The minute she'd seen him, she knew she'd stumbled onto Greer Delta, exactly as she'd prayed she would and by following her mysterious caller's map and very precise instructions. It was insane that she would walk right up to the one Delta she needed to find and he'd seemed to buy her story and agreed to shelter her so easily.

The crazier thing was ... she actually believed he wouldn't hurt her. There was something in his blue eyes that reassured her. She might live to regret her insanely brave quest, but it appeared that

Greer Delta was exactly as the Voice had promised her, a chivalrous cowboy and protector of women.

She still couldn't quite believe she was doing this. She'd gone back and forth arguing with herself and heaven all day after she'd talked to the Voice. Then two things had happened. The Navy had called and informed her Travis had gone AWOL and he'd been shot and killed during a "situation" they couldn't give her details about. Then they'd asked her where she wanted his body sent for burial.

It had confirmed exactly what the Voice had said would happen.

The second thing was the video from Travis. She'd read and re-read all the Voice's instructions and stared at the pile of money and prayed desperately to know what path she should take. It was all out of her league and terrifying. Then she finally got brave enough to watch the video her brother had asked the Voice to send to her. It was short, and it made her sob.

Travis had looked good. Strong, well-groomed, but far too serious. The video had been too brief, she'd wanted more. Travis had said, "Hi, sis. If you're watching this, I'm gone. I want you to know that I love you. You've known me my whole life, and you know I love my country. That I've sacrificed a lot for it. You've seen me overcome my demons, and you've inspired me with your purity and innocence. Stay strong, sis."

Then it cut off. Emery had cried then. She'd cried long and hard. When she'd finally stopped crying, she'd prayed, and she felt she had to do this. For Travis. For the country he'd loved and sacrificed for.

Everything had gone better than she could've planned. Now she could right the wrong done to her country and avenge her brother's death. Things seemed to be falling into place as if heaven above orchestrated them.

Thank you, she prayed. *Now please keep me safe and somehow able to keep lying convincingly to this man.*

After the graveside service yesterday afternoon, she'd kissed the

Weatherspoons goodbye and driven the ten hours from Salmon to Grand Junction, Colorado, stopping only to eat and get gas. She'd arrived early in the morning and crashed in a Motel 6, sleeping deeply and then waking about an hour later with the nightmare that had plagued her since she'd learned of Travis's death. Gruesome images of Travis killing a beautiful blonde woman who had ... Greer Delta's eyes.

Yikes, she was a mess.

It was after noon today when she'd found a place to store her car for a few weeks that took cash and didn't care what her name was. Her instructions from Mr. No-Name Compassionate Voice, aka the Voice, had said to use the cash and not leave her real name or a trace. He'd had a fake ID for her with Taylor Miles on it. He'd provided pictures of Greer Delta. Emery had studied the handsome cowboy's face, trying to assign malice and evil to the manly lines. It wasn't as easy as she'd hoped.

The Voice had claimed the Delta family had been deluded into believing their cause was good and right. If that was true, maybe that's why Growly Greer didn't look evil. Maybe the humble and good-looking cowboy wasn't evil, but simply misguided. He had only killed her brother because he'd been tricked into thinking Travis was the bad guy. It reassured her enough to take the plunge and try to vindicate her brother's death.

In the Voice's instructions was the promise that if she could find the location of the weapon, the Voice could take down the real bad guys, those who had assigned the Deltas to protect the weapon and had really caused Travis's death. So she'd tried to look at Greer Delta as a soldier following orders.

It was still disturbing being face to face with her brother's killer.

Apparently, his extended family owned an entire vale near the town of Summit Valley. The map was very detailed, showing the exact route she could hike from Summit Valley and arrive three hours later on the south end of the Deltas' land closest to Greer's home.

She'd paid an exorbitant amount to a cab driver in Grand Junction to drive her to Summit Valley and arrived early this afternoon. The cab had dropped her at the map's starting point and she'd started her trek across the mountains to their valley with only a small backpack with a couple thousand dollars in cash, travel-size makeup and toiletries, a water bottle, trail mix, clean underwear, shorts, socks, a T-shirt, and a can of bear spray. She prayed the entire time she wouldn't get eaten alive by a bear and that somehow, someway, she'd run into Greer Delta and he'd buy her story.

It had worked eerily well. Even with Greer not appearing to know who she was, looking to be a decent human being, and taking the bait, she was petrified to get too close to him. If she hadn't been so exhausted, dirty, and disheveled, she probably would've tried to hit him, scratch him, bite him, or at the very minimum give him an 'accidental' shot of the bear spray in her backpack. Lame rebuttals for him killing her brother, but she wasn't some expert at revenge. Wasn't it thirty years Inigo Montoya had sought to avenge his father's death and ten of those years he'd worked to become the greatest sword fighter in the world? She'd had like ten minutes to figure out how to get her revenge. Heaven help her, it would most likely go awry soon.

She wasn't sure if she was so nauseated because she hadn't eaten a proper meal in two days, because she was in the presence of her brother's killer and scared to death of how this operation would fail, or because of how conflicted she now felt about the man staring at her.

His blue eyes were clear and truthfully beautiful. If she didn't know who he was and what he'd done, she could've gotten lost in eyes that blue. She wanted to slap herself silly, but she couldn't stop looking at him and cataloguing a few other things that she'd seen in the pictures but was now being smacked in the face with.

His face was model handsome, with sculpted lines and a shadow of dark hair on his cheeks and strong jawline. The cowboy hat he wore was a nice compliment to his appeal, and his body was as impressive as his face. He filled out his T-shirt and jeans beautifully and was obviously a hard-working cowboy. Those defined muscles in his arms and under his T-shirt should've installed terror by their sheer size. She couldn't puzzle it out—and maybe she didn't want to—but those muscles looked comforting and attractive. He was tall, maybe six or seven inches taller than her five-foot-nine, and he wore it well.

In her fake role as Taylor, the escaping ex-girlfriend, she'd asked if he would protect her and if he would keep her safe. The Voice had claimed Greer Delta respected and protected women. Both times he'd simply said "yes" in a deep voice. He wasn't a man of many words, but there'd been something about that cowboy tone, his blue eyes, and his bearing. This man would protect her from anything and everything.

Was his serious cowboy demeanor why he'd agreed like he had, like it was a solemn vow between them, or was there something deeper going on, something she couldn't put her finger on? If the entire Delta family had been deluded into thinking they were working for the "good guys" but they really weren't, maybe the reason she'd felt impressed to come here was to help Greer and his family learn the truth. Maybe they could somehow help each other.

She shouldn't be so impressed and almost drawn to Greer Delta. She shouldn't want this man's protection. She should only want to hurt him like he'd hurt her. Instead, she found herself trusting that he would protect and help her. The only man she needed protection from was him, or maybe whoever his higher up was. It made no sense, and she was already sick of all the conflicting emotions battling inside of her. She was confused and tired and hungry. That was all. Her mind was too tired to even create synonyms.

She had to keep reminding herself that Greer Delta was a murderer who'd been indoctrinated to believe he was working for the good guys. It would probably be smart not to get caught in a staring contest with Mr. Blue Eyes Hypnotic Gaze as well. He might appear to be a hard-working cowboy, but she knew what he truly was. What he'd done. She had to stay sharp and leery while somehow gaining his trust.

Why had she agreed to this? She was a teacher and lover of books, especially The Princess Bride. She was *not* an actress, a special ops person, or resourceful, smart, and tough like Westley. She needed a Westley. Now there was a hero. Why was it Greer Delta appeared more attractive than Westley? Greer's eyes were as blue as Westley's. "With eyes like the sea after a storm," Buttercup had said.

Oh boy. No way could she go down that rabbit hole. She was living in an upside-down nightmare. The worst part was ... she'd put herself here.

No. The Voice, Greer and his family's actions, and even Travis had put her here. Now she'd better "act well thy part" or she could be in mortal danger.

Greer turned and reached out as if he would put his hand on her lower back to direct her toward his house. She flinched. Being close to him was hard enough. She didn't know that she could handle him touching her without going into berserk mode and blowing her cover the first five minutes she was with him.

Luckily, he clenched his fist and then brought it back to his side. He tilted his head. "This way."

She fell into step with him, wishing she had any clue what to say. The whole situation was so unprecedented she couldn't fault herself for feeling off-kilter. She was lying to her brother's killer and strangely felt ... comfortable. No way. Not possible. Inconceivable, unimaginable, ludicrous, implausible.

Oh, good—her brain was back on duty.

She couldn't possibly be comfortable around this guy or in her situation. Yet ... she snuck a glance at his strong profile. She might actually be ... not afraid of him. If only it wasn't him that had killed Travis. Greer exuded a calm strength and protectiveness that she'd craved her entire life. Her mind was a muddle of so many emotions and questions, but most of all trying to make sense of why she wasn't freaking out completely at this moment.

Greer said nothing. She appreciated that he could be quiet. Maybe he could hear her mind churning a million miles an hour and knew any words could push her over the edge of insanity, recklessness, foolishness, irrationality. It was like the Cliffs of Insanity. No one could ever survive that.

She shook her head at herself, and he looked askance at her. She pasted on a smile and kept striding forward. If she could've been able to push away the fact the man next to her had killed Travis, she would've enjoyed the quiet walk and the view of the gorgeous mountain valley with the lake in the middle and some homes and barns on the other side.

"Who lives over there?" she asked, pointing across the lake.

"My parents, Papa, and aunt and uncle."

"That's lucky you have family close."

He nodded. A few beats passed, and then he seemed to remember to reciprocate the conversation. There was too much intelligence in his eyes for him to be slow, but he sure didn't seem to like to talk. "Do you have ... family?"

She didn't let herself look at him, afraid she might scream that she would have family except for him, thank you very much, and "why don't you give me a nice paper cut and pour lemon juice in it"?

"No," she croaked out.

He said nothing.

They walked toward a sprawling house. The front door and porch faced the mountains, and the back faced the calm lake with a beautiful stretch of grass down to the water. They came in from a side door to the garage. It was a spacious area with a variety of residents that didn't fill the space. There was a nice four-door gray truck, a dirt bike, a side by side, a fancy Harley, and a black Tesla.

First of all, it was interesting Greer walked her in through a side door rather than show off that gorgeous front door of wood and glass that she'd glimpsed. Greer Delta apparently didn't put on airs, or at least wasn't trying to impress her. She glanced over at him, all relaxed and cowboy-ish, and decided it was that he wasn't trying to impress anyone. The thought wouldn't even cross his mind.

Second of all, she was distracted from all the angst and questions by the pressing question of why a tough guy cowboy would have a pretty boy car.

"Okay, all the macho man vehicles and toys fit," she said. "I have to admit I love the Harley, but ... a Tesla?"

He folded his arms across his chest and shrugged, a slight smile on his face. That face and upper body were impressive. Not that she was looking at him like that, or could ever be drawn to him. "Fun car."

She laughed. "A *fun car*? What if I went to ... your town, wherever that is, and told all the pretty girls that the tough, masculine cowboy Greer Delta drives an electric car?"

"Nobody would believe you." His slight smile turned into a smirk.

"Nobody would believe that Macho Man who can wrestle a steer to the ground is really a sissy who drives a Tesla and wears pink underpants?" She pressed her lips together. She was acting like one of her fourth-graders, but even worse, she was teasing with this man who should've been her enemy. He was her enemy. She needed to stop telling him he was tough and macho. Her tongue was always a mess. She had to somehow control it around this man.

He stared at her for half a second and then he laughed. It was a rich, deep chuckle that was so melodious and infectious she couldn't stop herself from laughing with him. They laughed together for a few seconds. It was freeing and fun and ... what was she doing laughing with this murderer? She abruptly stopped laughing and stared at him.

He stopped laughing as well, but he was still smiling.

"Sorry," she said, suddenly unable to meet his gaze, so she focused on the Tesla. "For a second there, I forgot ..." Her neck got hot, and she had no clue how she was going to keep up this façade. She'd forgotten who and what *he* was.

"About your ex chasing you," he prompted softly.

She let out a breath and made herself meet his blue eyes. She nodded quickly. "Yeah."

He studied her with compassion. "You're safe here," he said in a husky voice that just shouted protection.

Safe here from who? She wasn't sure who Greer believed he was protecting her from or who she needed protection from. The confusion was back and giving her a headache. Before she could tell him she was exhausted and beg him for a drink of water and a place to sleep, he quirked an eyebrow and asked, "Pink underpants?"

"I'll keep your secrets if you keep mine."

He smiled slightly, but then it disappeared. He studied her so intently she was certain he would tell her he knew she was lying, haul her to some Delta family torture chamber, and have them dissect her brain for information.

"Your secrets are safe," he said.

"Oh ... thank you." She had no clue what to think or feel at this moment. If she didn't know he was Greer Delta, she'd be intrigued and interested in him. But she did know, and that couldn't change. The fact that he'd killed Travis couldn't change.

A sudden flash of doubt filled her. What if the Voice was wrong? What if it wasn't Greer that had killed Travis? What if the Voice was lying? He had been right about Travis dying and the Navy saying he was AWOL. Was he right about Greer? Her head ached with all the questions and confusion.

He nodded, his lips in a firm line as he studied her. Looking for chinks in her armor, or was there a possibility he was attracted to her? No. She couldn't let herself feel an attraction to him.

"I'm about ready to pass out and I've got a headache. Can you show me where I'll be sleeping?"

His gaze deepened. He'd agreed she could stay until it was safe. Why did it feel like she was pushing her way into his home and his life? Maybe because she was.

"Sure."

He nodded and turned, gesturing for her to walk in front of him. He was too much of a gentleman. It fit with what the Voice had said, but it sure didn't fit with him being a cold-hearted killer. She shivered.

"Cold?" he asked. The concern in his deep voice sent a weird shiver through her. How did she explain she wasn't cold? She was completely out of her element, an emotional mess, and she wanted to hate his guts. Instead, she was drawn to him and completely confused by who or what he really was.

"No," she managed.

She walked up the garage steps and into a mudroom with an attached laundry and bathroom. White cabinets with gray and white swirled granite made for a bright, clean look.

He slipped off his boots and took off his cowboy hat, self-consciously brushing at his matted-down hair. It was odd to see him without the hat and in stocking-feet. It made him more approachable but also was too intimate. She looked away quickly. She could not let her mind go down forbidden paths like being intimate with Greer Delta.

"Excuse me," he murmured.

He walked into the bathroom and shut the door. Emery's shoulders lowered, and she felt like she could finally let her guard down. The water turned on, so she assumed he was washing his hands from being out doing chores or he was running water so she wouldn't hear him pee. She laughed out loud at that. As if Greer Delta would care what someone thought of him. He seemed far too tough and comfortable in his own skin.

Did he regret killing her brother?

That thought stopped her laughter. She shivered again and hugged herself. In the home of the growling Greer. She'd done it. She'd penetrated his evil lair. Now how to figure out where this secret weapon was so she could "bug out" like the voice had said and let the real soldiers do their job. She had no idea where to start. Break into his computer? Ask him? Sneak into his room at night and see if he sleep-talked or if she could find his phone, hold it up to his face, and read through all his info? One thing was certain: she wouldn't arm wrestle it out of him.

The water shut off and the door opened. Her breath rushed out like somebody had punched her. She had to keep reminding herself this wasn't a man she could trust or like. The problem was he radiated trustworthiness, like the most appealing boy scout you'd ever meet. And he seemed thoughtful and underspoken, which wasn't a word, but she liked those qualities. Especially as she often rushed ahead and spoke too much.

"Wash up?" he asked.

It was funny how he didn't waste any words. She stared at him. "You don't talk much, do you?"

He shook his head.

"That's nice. I can talk enough for the both of us."

He smiled at that.

She hurried through the bathroom door so she didn't do something crazy like touch him. It was bad enough that she'd smiled at him, laughed with him, and thought he was attractive.

Greer Delta was the enemy. She had to remember that.

But for some insane reason, he didn't feel like the enemy. That scared her as much as anything.

She turned the water on so she could pee without him hearing her. It made her laugh. Oh my, she was either on the verge of a breakdown or had entered an alternate reality.

Chapter Four

Greer paced in the living room waiting for Emery or Taylor or whoever she was to come out of the bathroom. He was suspicious and edgy and crazily attracted to a woman he had no right to be attracted to.

He needed to call Papa and see what his advice was. If anyone could do it, Papa could muddle Greer out of this mess. He was confused. Emery was not only incredibly appealing to him but had made him smile and ... laugh. He didn't even know what to think about that. Only his hilarious little brother Hudson and his cousin Maddie could make him laugh.

He rubbed at his chest. If the beautiful woman in his bathroom really was Emery Reeder and had come here to avenge her brother or attempt to steal the secret, it would hurt down deep. He'd barely met her, so that was as insane as him laughing at her little comments.

He heard the bathroom door open, and then Emery walked into the main living area. Her warm brown eyes focused on him for a moment, and warmth filled his chest. She quickly looked away. Her gaze swept around his spacious great room, seeming to catalog the vaulted ceilings, hickory cabinets, gray granite countertops, leather furniture, distressed cherry floor, and floor to ceiling windows overlooking the lake and mountains beyond. It was growing dark, so the picture-perfect lake was a deep, dusky blue.

"Your house is gorgeous," she murmured.

"Thank you." He was proud of his sprawling rambler. His cousin Alivia had designed and built it for him. The same cousin he'd protected while shooting this woman's brother. A tremor went through him at the thought. *Please don't let her be Emery Reeder*, he begged heaven above, though he was ninety-nine percent certain she was. It was hard enough trying to forgive himself for Reeder's violent end. This twist of the man's sister appearing in Greer's world and staying in his house was too much. Especially if the angels above had directed her here.

They stared at each other and he tried to remember the manners his mom had drilled into him. "Hungry?" he grunted out.

"Yes, but I'm more tired than hungry," she said.

Did that mean he should feed her or not? He was the furthest thing from a host. He rubbed at his jaw. "A snack?"

"No, thanks. I can eat tomorrow. I'd love to steal a bottle of water and climb into bed."

"Okay." That he could handle.

He hurried to the fridge, grabbed a bottle of water, and brought it back to her. As he handed it over, it happened. Their fingers brushed. Warmth erupted from the simple touch of her skin, and he froze. Their gazes collided and he could see that same warmth lighting up her beautiful brown eyes.

Then Greer did the craziest thing he'd ever done. Instead of moving away, he wrapped his hand around hers.

She startled and stared at him as if she could see into his soul. Greer felt like she was a grounding wire and he was being struck by lightning. The sensation was intense and warm and should've been painful, but she grounded and protected him.

Yanking her hand free, she stepped back and held up the water bottle. "Thanks so much," she said far too brightly. "Where do you want me to sleep? I can sleep on the couch if you need."

"No," he managed, feeling completely out of sorts, not from the way it felt to touch her, but from her pulling away.

He gestured her to the south. On the north side of his house, his master suite had views east and west. The great room was in the middle with the large living area, kitchen, and dining room. The entryway and his office were at the front of the house. On the south side, behind the garage, was a workout room and two spare bedrooms with a bathroom between them. One bedroom had nothing in it, but Esther, Alivia, Maddie, and Jessie insisted he have the third room done up for "guests." He would've scoffed at them, but Greer wasn't much of a scoffer. Needless to say, he'd lived in the house for three years and Esther, Maddie, and Jessie, had each stayed in the room once, probably to make him feel like it hadn't been a complete waste of money but not overwhelm him with too much human interaction. His sister and cousins would be ecstatic to know he had a female guest. Until they found out who it was.

They walked through the living area and he reached in front of her to push open the guest bedroom door. She looked around at the four-poster bed, nightstand, and large windows overlooking the lake.

Greer walked past her and opened the closet. He lifted out a set of clean sheets and said, "Nobody's slept in the bed. Might be dusty." It was a lot of words for him. He'd talked more around her than he did around anyone. She didn't move, and he didn't know if he should change out the sheets or leave them for her.

"I don't think it matters," she said, gesturing to herself. "I'm a dirty mess."

He looked her over. She was dirty except for her face, arms, and hands that she'd scrubbed in the mud room bathroom. He held up a finger, then turned and strode from the room. Hurrying through the house, he went to his master, grabbed a T-shirt out of his closet, and rushed back to the guest room. Emery hadn't moved.

He handed over the T-shirt, careful to not brush her hand and risk losing his mind again. "Shower and sleep in this," he pushed out. "I can wash your clothes."

She looked him over. The warmth he'd felt in his chest spread to his extremities. She was attracted to him, and the thought made him ... lightheaded. Greer always thought of himself as strong, but right now he felt so weak he was tempted to lean against the doorframe.

Emery shook out the T-shirt. Her brow furrowed and her mouth curved into a smile. What shirt had he given her? It just looked like one of his plain gray T-shirts.

"'I never dreamed I'd be a super sexy rancher, but here I am killin' it,'" she read aloud, turning the shirt around so he could see the print on the front.

Greer froze. "Um ..."

She looked up at him and laughed. "And here I thought you were a humble guy."

"My cousin," he pushed out by way of explanation. He closed his eyes and shook his head. Maddie. She'd given him the shirt for Christmas, thinking she was hilarious. He'd thanked her. And had never worn it.

Looking at Emery again, he shook his head and muttered, "Sorry." He held out his hand for the shirt. He'd go exchange it for one that had no writing on it.

She pulled the shirt into her chest and shook her head. "It's mine now. Finders keepers, losers weepers."

He couldn't help but laugh. He rarely cared to say much, but at the moment, he had no idea what to say.

Her pretty cheeks flushed darker, and she backed toward the bed. "Sorry, I spend a lot of time with nine- and ten-year-olds."

Greer's laughter cut off. What age did Emery Reeder teach? He should grill this Emery slash Taylor person and dig to the truth, but talking to Papa first was probably the better route.

"Leave your clothes." He pointed to the door, then hurried toward it.

"Thank you," she said.

He turned around to nod at her.

"I'm so grateful you're putting me up and protecting me." She put a hand to her heart and said in a falsely low-pitched voice, "'Thank you from the bottom of my cold, dark heart.'"

Greer almost laughed again. Where did she come up with this stuff? But then it hit him. Her cold, dark heat. If she was Emery Reeder as he feared, her heart would be cold, dark, and angry because of him.

He lifted his chin and pulled the door shut behind him. Yanking his cell phone out, he could not stand to wait one more second. He hurried into his bedroom, shut and locked the door, and then into his bathroom. He shut and locked that door also, and turned on the shower for good measure. He pressed a button and within seconds he heard, "Greer?"

"Papa," he breathed out. "Emery Reeder ... my guest room."

"What?" Papa's voice was a mixture of confusion and concern.

Greer explained, answering Papa's questions and giving any info he could think of, using up more oxygen and vocal cords than he'd wasted in a lot of years. As he finished, Papa didn't speak for a second, then he said, "Okay, I'll do some research and let you know what I find in the morning. Meanwhile, you should probably sleep with your door locked and a loaded gun under your pillow."

"Papa." He was surprised. Papa and his dad had taught him to always respect and protect women.

"I'm just saying," Papa said. "If that is Emery Reeder, she has more reason to hate you and do you harm than anyone you know."

Greer pushed out a breath. Papa was right, but he didn't think that beautiful woman could hurt anyone.

"Your smoke alarms are functioning?" Papa asked.

"Yes."

"She could disable the ones in the main area, but you have some in your bedroom and bathroom. Should I set alarms to come check on you?"

"No." Greer had been suspicious of her, and he had every right to be, but he felt instinctively protective of her. He didn't like Papa assuming she was some murderer.

"What about a bomb? You said she had a backpack. Do you think you can check it after she falls asleep?"

"No." That woman wouldn't blow him up or burn him in his sleep. How he knew that, he wasn't certain, but he did.

"I'm worried, Greer. Why would she be there? How would she march across the mountains and somehow show up right where you are? Is she after vengeance, or maybe whoever hired Travis Reeder and his buddies recruited her because they failed?" Greer had wondered the same things. "Hmm. I think you should get out of there. Come stay here and you can go back home in the morning before she wakes up."

"No, Papa."

"No?"

"She's ... good. I promise." Some people thought he was slow because of how little he spoke, but Papa didn't. Papa had told me many times he was smarter than most because he chose his words carefully and didn't waste his or other people's time talking too much. Papa was great, but he was wrong in thinking Emery could hurt Greer. Greer had wondered the same thing initially, if she was going to shove a knife through his heart. In the short time he'd spent with her, he knew she was innocent and pure and was probably being used by someone.

Papa pushed out a heavy breath. "How do you know?"

How *did* he know? This woman could be playing him for every kind of fool, but unless she was the actress of the year, he didn't buy it. He'd seen her goodness, her kindness, her sense of humor. She'd been wary around him, but she wasn't capable of hurting someone. He just knew it.

"Her eyes," he finally admitted. The new Tyler Hubbard song played in his head: *Five-foot-nine, brown eyes, in a sundress.* Emery had been in shorts and a T-shirt. She didn't need a sundress to be beautiful.

"Ah, Greer. Please don't fall for a pretty pair of eyes and get yourself killed."

"I won't."

Papa waited, but Greer wouldn't run from Emery and go stay at Papa's house. He somehow trusted she wouldn't try to kill him. He had no idea why she was here, but he did know her story of being Taylor, running from her ex, and somehow ending up at his ranch didn't add up. He was ninety-nine-point-nine percent certain she was Emery Reeder. He was also ninety-five percent sure she wouldn't set him on fire in the night.

The five percent doubt should worry him more.

When he said nothing more, Papa finally grunted, "I'll have everybody set alarms and come check on you."

"Please ... nobody else." He didn't need the entire family knowing about Emery. Not yet. He had to let Papa dig through his intel and then somehow figure this out with Emery first. She might be the key to the information they needed about who'd hired Travis Reeder and his buddies. Not that he would use Emery for info, but maybe when she trusted him she would willingly share. It might take a while for her to learn to fully trust him.

Papa groaned. "You realize I'm old and need my sleep."

"Sleep, please."

"You know I won't. Love you, son. Be smart. I'll be praying and I'll be checking on you."

"Love you," he pushed out. He loved his grandfather. It was just hard to say those words.

The phone clicked off. Greer stared at it. Then he peeled off his dirty clothes, dropped them in the hamper, and climbed in the shower. He rested his head against the granite tile. His thoughts bounced around, wondering why Emery was here, what she knew about him and her brother's death, and the slim hope that she really was Taylor and not Emery.

He groaned in frustration. It was a really slim hope, and it was going to be a really long night.

Chapter Five

Emery felt shaky and off kilter as she looked at the bedroom door Greer Delta had just shut behind him. Greer Delta. He didn't growl. He didn't even feel growly. How could that quiet, confident, appealing cowboy be her brother's murderer? It didn't add up. When he'd touched her hand, she felt warm and like she'd come home. That made no sense. If that hand had truly killed Travis, Emery was horrified by her reaction.

She dug her fingertips into her forehead. She'd never been so confused. Dropping the T-shirt Greer had given her on the bed, she sank into a cozy armchair and watched the night deepen. The gorgeous lake and mountains beyond were picture perfect. Her life sure wasn't. Her life was a mess.

Unzipping the backpack, she pulled out her phone and texted the Voice's number. *I'm in. He seemed to buy the story.*

Great, the guy responded quickly. *Figure out the location and let me know. Your brother will be so proud and your nation grateful.*

She responded with a thumbs up, but rather than feeling gratified by the man's empty praise, irritation laced through her. Was she crazy? Had she really felt impressed from heaven above and Travis's video to come here? She was starting to doubt heavenly inspiration. She was insane to have agreed to infiltrate Greer's life.

All that money and the Voice's continuous reminders about her serving her country like Travis would have done and avenging her brother's death had made her feel like she was committed without ever agreeing to it. A tick of fear said the Voice could be lying and using her for his own agenda against the Delta family. What did she know? The only facts she had were that Travis was definitely dead and the Navy had definitely said he was AWOL and hadn't admitted that his death had anything to do with a special ops mission or any mission associated with the military. That part of the story backed up the Voice being truthful. Travis would never go AWOL. The military was his life, and she wanted to serve her country and finish the job Travis had started.

But Greer ... that man had thrown a wrench in her plans. He appeared to be all things good, humble, kind, and attractive. The Voice had said the Deltas had been deluded into believing they were representing the good guys. So Greer might be deluded and have every good intention of doing what was right. In his head, he could believe he'd killed her brother for the greater good. Yet could Greer be a killer? He sure didn't seem like it.

She shoved the phone back into her backpack, pulled out her toiletry kit, stood, and picked up the T-shirt. She wanted to smell it and see if it smelled like Greer. As if she knew what he smelled like. She could imagine he smelled like leather, horses, outdoors, and musk. A real manly, macho, masculine, tough, appealing smell.

"Ugh," she grunted at herself. Who cared what he smelled like? She could not be attracted to him. That was all kinds of twisted.

She hurried to strip out of her T-shirt and shorts. She was tempted to leave her bra and panties outside the door for Greer to launder as well. That made her smile. He'd be so embarrassed. She hardly knew him, but she knew touching her bra and panties would flip him out.

She gently slid open the door and dropped her T-shirt and shorts outside of it. There was a shower running somewhere in the house. Shutting the door, she hurried to the bathroom attached to her bedroom, locking the doors leading to both bedrooms and the hallway. The shower felt wonderful, and she scrubbed at her own underwear and hung them in the shower to dry. Luckily she had extra clothes in her backpack—not that Greer knew that. Did he suspect who she was? He had to. There'd been flashes of something suspicious in his eyes several times as they'd talked, but he'd been a complete gentleman throughout their interaction.

How many people would invite some supposedly abused and afraid stranger into their house? Not many. If he believed she was Taylor, he was an impressive protector of women. If he realized she was Emery, he was probably subscribing to the theory to keep your enemies close. She really didn't want to be his enemy, but her loyalty to Travis demanded it.

She pulled on her clean underwear and then tugged Greer's shirt over her head. It smelled like clean laundry. That made sense as he'd probably never worn a shirt that said he was a "super sexy rancher." She smiled, thinking how his tanned skin had grown darker as she'd read those words aloud.

Wiping the smile off her face, she dropped to her knees and prayed for help. She was so confused. Was the Voice a good guy and helping her avenge her brother or was Greer a good guy and the Voice was using her or did Greer just *think* he was a good guy like the Voice had explained?

She had no idea and even prayer didn't settle her. She had felt impressed to come here; she was sure of it. She'd cling to that and go forward with faith. Her gut turned over with worry. A lot of faith.

She hurried to change the sheets and dropped the old ones outside the door as well. She felt bad having Greer do her laundry. But that was stupid. She shouldn't feel badly about any of this. Her brother was dead and the Voice was certain Greer had killed him. She should be terrified and angry, but she was more unsettled and baffled and so, so sad. Ah, Travis. She dropped to her knees once again and prayed for his soul and for her protection and to somehow see clearly through this muddle.

Standing, she trudged to the bathroom again. She brushed her wet hair and her teeth, used the bathroom, checked to make sure the bedroom door and door to the bathroom from her bedroom was locked, and then stretched out on the clean sheets. It felt nice. These were high-quality sheets and a high-quality bed and pillow. Maybe she'd go a night without the nightmare.

Should she stay awake and go search through Greer's office for any clues about the secret weapon? Would his computer be password-protected? If he was hiding something, it probably would. Maybe she could get his phone from his nightstand, hold it up to his sleeping face to unlock it, and read through texts and emails until she found the answers the Voice needed so she could get out of this confusing chaos.

Both ideas sounded terrifying. If he caught her, what would she say and what would he do? No matter the voice saying Greer wouldn't hurt a lady and her own instinctive feelings that he was a complete gentleman. He'd killed her brother to protect this weapon. She had to keep reminding herself Greer could be very dangerous, though he hadn't felt dangerous to her.

She groaned. She was insane. How had she thought she could fish out some secret from a highly trained killer? What was she doing here?

Rolling over, she squeezed her eyes shut and prayed over and over again. "Help me. Please help me."

She was pushing through a forest. It was thick and dark and eerie.

Travis's voice echoed through the air. "Tell me the secret. Lead me to the weapon!"

Emery ran toward him, stopping at the edge of a clearing and screaming in horror as her brother pulled out a knife and stabbed a blonde woman repeatedly. The woman cried out in anguish, her blue eyes full of pain and horror. Blood gushed from her wounds.

"No!" Emery screamed. "Travis, no! Stop!"

Great sobs shook her body. Travis wouldn't murder some woman. He couldn't. He was a good person. He'd protected and been there for Emery.

"No!" she screamed over and over. "No, stop! Travis, stop!"

"Taylor. Taylor."

Someone was touching her shoulder and kept repeating the name Taylor. That made about as much sense as her awful dream.

"Wake up." The voice was masculine and deep. It rumbled through her and gave her a sense of peace.

Emery's eyes fluttered open. She was on a bed, tangled in the sheets. The room was dimly lit by a glow coming in through the open door. She looked up into the handsome face of Greer Delta. His blue eyes were full of concern.

"You okay?" he asked softly.

"No," she managed. She wasn't okay; she was a blubbering mess. A sob ripped from her throat and her body trembled. Travis was dead. His alleged killer being so kind and appealing was messing with her head. She was out of her element in this house and this entire situation. The nightmare disturbed her even more than it had each night she'd had it this past week. It felt like that forest and some outside elements she couldn't place were dangerous and they were coming for her. Travis was gone and couldn't watch out for her any longer.

The only thing that seemed real and safe was this man studying her with such concern. The worry in his blue eyes deepened as she blubbered and completely fell apart.

The last person she should trust was the one her heart told her she could. That was seriously messed up.

She'd had a few therapeutic cries since Travis had died, but not like this. Heaving sobs shook her body and she couldn't get control of herself.

"Don't cry," Greer murmured softly.

She tried, but she couldn't stop. Her lip trembled and the tears ran down her face and she was humiliated that this tough man was watching her cry. She wanted the nightmare she'd just had, but more importantly the nightmare her life had become, to go away. Right now.

Please, right now, she begged heaven above. *Let me close my eyes and just disappear. Beam me back to Nevada. I'll take heat and sagebrush over having Greer Delta see me cry.*

Greer sank onto the bed next to her and gently reached out to her, shoving thoughts of disappearing completely from her mind.

He softly patted her shoulder, and the look on his face was priceless. This big, rough cowboy was completely discomfited by a woman crying in his presence. He obviously wanted to comfort and help her but had no idea how. It was so awkwardly endearing.

Emery's crying calmed, and she stared at him. His presence and warm, musky smell overwhelmed her in a very good way. But it was his inept patting that was oddly comforting and so sweet. Most men as handsome and confident in their own skin as Greer Delta were probably masters at charming a woman. But Greer had absolutely no idea how to charm or comfort her. It made her strangely happy. This cowboy could probably have any woman in the world chasing him, but he didn't seem to know that. He was definitely *not* a womanizer, and she doubted he had much experience with women.

Their gazes locked, and his hands settled on her shoulders. The pressure of those large palms filled her with an unfamiliar warmth. He slowly slid his large palms around to her upper back and gently tugged her against his broad chest.

Sighing, she cuddled in against him, laid her head on his muscular shoulder, and wrapped her arms around his back. His T-shirt was soft, but his body was very, very firm.

He didn't say or do anything; he simply held her. Emery had never felt anything to equal his warm, safe, protective embrace.

She instinctively knew that she needed Greer Delta—his touch, his comfort, his ability to protect her. Against all rational sense, this man seemed to be her shelter amid a lightning and thunderstorm. The storm was pummeling her with stinging wind and rain, terrifying her with loud claps of thunder, and threatening to singe her with lightning bolts. None of that could touch her in Greer's arms.

This man wouldn't hurt her. He wouldn't hurt anyone.

Several beautiful moments passed as he cuddled her close and she clung to him before the lightning bolt hit her right in the middle of her traitorous forehead.

What in the name of the minions of the underworld am I thinking?

She jolted and scurried away from him, her back slamming painfully into the headboard behind her as reality knocked her for a loop.

This man had killed her brother. What was she *doing* hugging him? Worse, what was she doing thinking he could be her shelter, comfort, solace, protection, safeguard, possibly her everything? She was insane and she deserved to be hit by lightning. Struck dead so she could join Travis and beg his forgiveness.

They stared at each other in the softly lit room.

His blue eyes were full of compassion and worry. "You okay?"

"No," she admitted.

He looked like he wanted to reach for her again, but she could not let that happen. He was her shelter from the storm? Had she completely lost it? He'd *caused* the storm.

Unless the Voice was lying to her and using her. Could he have fabricated his information? He couldn't have fabricated the video from Travis. What agenda would some unknown man have to put her in Greer Delta's house and life? Obviously he wanted that weapon. Was Emery just a tool for him? Had Travis been the Voice's pawn?

Oh man, her head hurt.

Greer waited as if she'd talk it out. It almost made her smile; he seemed to be the last person who wanted to talk about anything. If only she could trust Greer enough to beg for some Excedrin and then spill the entire story. She'd love to rely on him, hear his side of things, let him help her sort everything out. Maybe they could help each other.

No! There was no way she was confiding in him. He might claim innocence and kill her in her sleep or tell her yes, he'd killed her brother and now it was her turn to meet her Redeemer. It was a good thing she had faith and believed in a merciful and loving Father above. Even so, she wasn't quite ready to dash off to the pearly gates.

Right now she needed to sleep and think. She needed time and lots of heavenly help to sort out this mess. She also needed distance from his inviting arms while somehow getting to know him well enough to figure out who she could trust. She was living in a nightmare as bad as the recurring one she'd just had.

"Please ..." She grasped for some excuse. "My head is pounding like an eighties heavy metal band. I need to sleep. Sorry I woke you."

He simply nodded and stood. He moved with fluid strength and she had to look away to stop that rush of warm feelings from returning. How fickle was she?

Her gaze caught on the open bedroom door. She distinctly remembered locking it.

"How did you get in here?" she asked.

"Picked the lock," he said matter-of-factly, like everybody picked locks. "You were screaming," he added, as if that justified him picking her lock and entering her bedroom.

He hadn't stopped there, now had he? Greer had come into her room and then he'd given her a hug for the record books. He'd held her protectively, warmly, beautifully. His arms around her had briefly fulfilled every dream she'd ever had of being safe and wanted by an incredible man, of having a place in life, a home and a family.

She shook her head to stop her thoughts. She wasn't safe here—far from it. Her brother's murderer could come into her bedroom anytime he wanted. Shuddering, she looked away from his searching gaze.

"Screaming is actually good practice for my vocal cords," she said. "So next time you hear a cacophony of desperate screams, could you please put some earbuds in, turn that sad country music song up loud enough to damage your cochlea, and just let me have a cathartic scream and cry session?"

He let out a surprised laugh, and she couldn't stop herself from staring at him. She liked making him laugh. Then their gazes met and got all tangled up.

His mirth died, and his blue eyes focused so completely on her she felt like she might be Greer Delta's heart's desire. The depth of that gaze had her panting for air. Whatever Greer thought or knew about her as Emery or Taylor, he was definitely attracted to and interested in her and he liked that she made him laugh. The connection she felt to him made her tremble. She clutched her hands together and gave him a pointed and saucy look. She didn't want him to leave, but she sure needed him to or she'd never get her head on straight.

Holding up his hands as if in surrender, he backed toward the door. She was glad he was going. Kind of. She was glad he wouldn't come if she had another nightmare and screamed herself hoarse. But that was an outright lie. She hated the nightmare and would love to have those strong arms around her again, feel that sense of safety and home and warmth.

At that moment, he did something that was almost as disarming and incredible as his touch earlier had been and his gaze now was.

He smiled.

It was a beautiful, full smile that took his face from perfectly handsome to sculpted by angels.

She smiled back. She couldn't stop herself.

For several beautiful seconds, they simply smiled at each other. Then he nodded to her and murmured, "Night."

"Goodnight," she returned. She wanted to thank him for waking her up, for holding her, for showing her that an embrace could be the safety, warmth, and home she'd always longed for.

Instead, she watched him go. Then she sank into the pillow and didn't move. The living room light shut off, and she heard his bedroom door shut. She didn't bother shutting hers. What was the point? He'd pick the lock anyway.

A delicious shiver went through her. Greer Delta was incredible, and she was staying in his house.

The shiver turned icy cold. Could he possibly be a murderer and a fraud? What if he was lulling her into thinking he was a great guy? He might be trying to get the information out of her about why she was here. As soon as he had that information, he'd shoot her in the head like he had her brother.

What kind of person could shoot someone in the head? It was vicious and final and terrifying. No coming back from that one. Travis wasn't coming back. Emery was alone. And sleeping in the house of her mortal enemy.

Emery stared at the open doorway. Her stomach twisted and her eyes burned as she tried to see through the darkness. Was Greer's heart dark and twisted? Did he think he was fighting for the good guys like the Voice had said? Was it possible he didn't realize he'd killed an innocent man on a secret ops mission for the U.S. Navy? What if the Voice was lying and either Greer hadn't been the one who'd killed her brother or Travis was the one who'd been deluded and on a mission for the bad guys?

She couldn't reason it out tonight. It was impossible to make any of it fit perfectly in her head. She liked to solve puzzles and make things fit, and she had no idea how to do that tonight.

And she didn't dare close her eyes.

Chapter Six

Greer hardly slept. He wasn't certain if Taylor was truly Emery Reeder and planning to stab him while he slept, or if there was a crazy miracle and he'd just been given a gift straight from heaven of the most appealing, smart, and hilarious woman he'd ever encountered begging him to shelter and protect her.

When he'd drifted off initially last night, he'd awoken to her screaming, "help" and "no" alternately. He'd debated at her door for too long, but he couldn't take the screams any longer and had quickly picked the lock to get in. Then he'd been rewarded with the opportunity of a lifetime ... holding her. He couldn't recall any woman who had hugged or even kissed him setting off that level of protectiveness and desire inside his chest, even Belinda. There was a warmth that filled him and lingered even after Taylor had removed herself from his arms.

He woke at five a.m. as usual to feed and water the sick herd and the new calves and check on his cattle. In the summer, the healthy cows ate grass or foraged in the fields. In the winter, he had to keep grass feeding them as the meat fetched a higher-price with "grass-finished" on the label.

Before he headed out, he couldn't stop himself from easing across the living area and peeking into the guest bedroom. Why had she left the door open when she'd seemed upset that he'd picked her lock and come into her room last night?

He told himself he was only checking to make sure his guest was all right, but when he saw that angelic face resting against the white pillowcase with her dark curls spread out like a halo, he had to rub at his chest to work out the knot that suddenly formed.

Please don't let her be Emery Reeder, he begged heaven above. He could sense it was an empty prayer, but he couldn't stop himself from praying it.

Backing away, he hurried out through the garage, slipping into his boots and putting his hat on his head. He went through his chores on auto-pilot, wondering how long it would take Papa to get the information on Taylor slash Emery. Then he started wondering how late she would sleep, planning what he'd cook her for breakfast, wondering if he could hug her again today, and trying to figure out what he'd do with a plus-one all day long.

He was riding Bear along the fence line, luckily seeing no sign of breaks in the barbed wire or animal attacks from last night on the older calves tagging along with their mother cows, when his phone rang.

"Papa," he greeted. He was instantly alert, and no matter how he wanted to ignore it, worried. He wanted Emery to be Taylor, wanted it badly. He'd shelter her from her ex, get to know her, someday in the future kiss her, then when he had her permission he'd set up a trap, lure the ex in, and dismantle the guy, then he'd kiss Taylor some more. He'd never had such an exciting and out-of-the-norm vision.

"You can imagine there are dozens of Taylor Miles in America.

We narrowed it down based on age and proximity and we've found her."

Greer pulled in a breath, praying for good news.

"Taylor Miles is a twenty-seven-year-old elementary school teacher from Denver, Colorado, teaching fourth grade at Park Hill Elementary," Papa began.

Greer almost punched a fist in the air and cheered, but of course he'd never do that. He waited for more info. Interesting; she was actually a year older than him.

"Her online photos bear an uncanny resemblance to Emery Reeder."

So that fit as well.

"The problem is the photos are all of her alone. No family. No friends."

That was sad but she'd told him she had no one.

"And that's not where the holes in the story end."

Ah, crap. His dream started sliding sideways.

"My resources started checking into things last night and they can't find a single person who knows Taylor Miles. Her picture and bio are on the elementary's website, but so far everybody they've contacted associated with the school has no idea who Taylor is."

Greer's chest felt tight, the complete opposite of how warm and expanded it had felt last night.

"Granted, it's only six-thirty in the morning, but they had a couple hours last night to get responses. We'll keep digging, but ..."

"She's Emery Reeder." A heaviness descended on him, and he hunched over the saddle horn. He had to face the facts. Emery Reeder had plowed through the forest to find him and try to trick him with a fabricated story. There was only one reason she'd do that. She knew he'd killed her brother and she wanted revenge. She was probably after the secret as well. Had Travis told her his plans before his death, or had whoever hired Travis gone after Emery to finish their dirty work?

It hurt to have his dreams destroyed. No matter how little he'd truly believed in them.

"Looks like it. I don't like this, Greer. Hypervigilant doesn't even begin to describe what you need to be. I'd come remove her from your house right now, but we need to know what information she has, why she's here, and if she's part of Travis's puppeteer's plan to find out where the secret is. I doubt she'll tell me anything if I blow her cover and interrogate her."

Greer's gut wrenched. He didn't want Papa interrogating her. He wanted to protect her. He'd promised to protect her. He just hadn't known at the time he'd be protecting her from his own family.

Bear kept trotting along the property line and Greer attempted to look for vulnerable spots in the fence or danger to his cattle. All he could see was Emery's gorgeous and innocent-seeming brown eyes in his mind.

"Here's what I have on Emery Reeder's recent activities," Papa continued. "She left the home of her foster parents in Salmon, Idaho two days ago. Her 1998 Accord was parked in a storage unit in Grand Junction, Colorado yesterday morning. She paid cash for the unit and asked the owner not to put a name down. She hasn't used a credit or debit card in almost a week, hasn't taken a withdrawal from her bank account, and she paid cash for her brother's funeral. On her teacher's salary, and with her just buying a house and using her savings for the down payment, I can't imagine she has a surplus of cash hiding under her mattress. If she did she'd upgrade her car. The Navy officer who informed her of her brother's death said she seemed strangely detached and not at all surprised Travis Reeder was dead and asked no questions when informed that he was AWOL. The school where she works said she was teaching summer school, but in light of her brother's death they gave her the rest of the summer off. Your thoughts?"

"Someone gave her cash and info to avenge her brother or keep up the hunt for the secret. Maybe both." Greer took a quick breath. All these long sentences in the last twelve hours were getting to him.

"Exactly." Papa exhaled. "I still see no indicators that she's violent, but if she knows you killed Travis and whoever paid her has set her up with weapons, as well as their twisted version of events and a surplus of cash, you could be in extreme danger."

"She's not dangerous." His voice felt tight and not just because he rarely used it. Whatever Emery Reeder was, whatever information she might have or quest she might be on, that woman could never hurt someone.

"You don't know that, Greer." Papa sounded tired. "Please be careful. I've seen the pictures. I know she looks beautiful and innocent, and she might be, but the fact remains she has to hate you for killing her brother and somebody has to be helping her. My gut says it's the same person or persons who sent Ensigns Reeder, Newman, and Wright after the secret and paid them a million up front and the promise of five million if they succeeded. Those men were willing to resort to kidnapping, violence, and murder to succeed. Whoever hired them will not stop."

It was all bad. Really bad for the family, for the Delta secret, for their nation. Greer had never thought of himself as selfish, but right now all he could think was how bad this was for him personally. Taylor was in fact Emery, his dream woman didn't exist, and in Papa's words, she had to hate him for killing her brother. Of course she did. How would he feel if someone had killed Aiden, Hudson, or Chandler? If someone had so much as hurt his sister Esther? One of his cousins? He'd avenge them.

His gut was churning and all thoughts of eating a relaxed breakfast, talking more than he ever had, and working his way into more hugs with Taylor sadly disappeared. She was Emery, and an incredible actress.

"Here's what I'm thinking," Papa continued. "You keep pretending you think she's Taylor. You keep her close and see if you can get her to trust you somehow, get any information you can out of her."

Greer hated all of this. He wanted to grow close to Emery, but not to ferret information out of her. How would she ever forgive him for killing her brother, and how could he ever trust her?

"You're out riding Bear?"

"Yep."

"Okay. Get back home, make her breakfast, and then get her out of the house. With her cover story, she claims she wants to stay hidden, right? See if she'll go on a horseback ride, a boat ride, a hike, whatever you can think of. Reassure her it'll just be the two of you and your family pretty much leaves you to yourself. I'll make sure everybody knows not to stop by."

Oh, great. First, he was going to lie; his family came to visit far more than was necessary. His mom always worried that he was an introvert and was going to "grow old alone." Second, Greer was not the type to entertain anybody.

"I'll watch your house with binoculars for you to leave. Plan on being out by ten if you can. Thor and I will get in there quick and get cameras with sensors set up. Check her bag for weapons."

"No cameras in her bedroom," Greer grunted out.

"Of course not. We'll put them in the living area. She has to cross that to get to your room. I'll send you an app and logins for your phone and an alarm will sound between ten p.m. and six a.m. if there's movement. You'll know and we'll know. If she goes to attack you, you can defend yourself and we'll get there fast."

Was that necessary? He trusted Papa, so he just said, "Kay."

"All right. I'll keep researching and we'll see if Miss Reeder reveals anything to you or if whoever is behind all this makes another move. Everything's been quiet since Alivia and Klein's foiled kidnapping. We'll keep our patrols around the cave, but you're off that detail for now. Esther's taking a leave of absence from the Air Force to help out, Maddie said she'd work from here for a while, and Jessie is still on summer break, so we have enough coverage."

Greer nodded even though Papa couldn't see him. His sister and cousins were as well trained as he was and would do a great job.

"What do you need, Greer? How else can I help you?" Papa's voice was kind and understanding. He knew Greer wasn't given to excessive emotion, but shooting Travis Reeder had been devastating to him. Now it was hitting him harder than ever with Emery Reeder coming into his life. He had no idea how to navigate or deal with any of it.

"Prayer," he grunted.

"Of course. I'll send out a prayer request to the family and if you need to talk, I'm always here."

"Thanks."

"I'm sorry this is all happening to you, but ... I see God's hand in it. You asked me how you could help Emery Reeder. Maybe this crazy turn of events can somehow bring peace to both of your hearts. Maybe she's confused, and surely she's hurting. Hopefully you can help her somehow."

Greer had no clue how peace or helping Emery could happen, but he wasn't about to argue with Papa. Especially when he'd felt heaven's hand yesterday when Emery walked into his life.

"I'm always so proud of you. You are one hundred percent loyal, kind, and good to the bone. I love you," Papa said in a deep voice filled with emotion.

Greer found himself choked up. He knew his grandfather, parents, and family loved him and thought he was a good person, but only his mom and Esther told him they loved him every other minute, though they'd both claim it was only once a week or so. To hear Papa say those words meant a lot. He didn't feel like a good-to-the-bone person right now. His worries over Emery, and how to somehow help her without endangering his family and the secret they'd been tasked to protect, was overwhelming.

"Love you," he managed. Twice in two days now, he'd said those words to Papa. He tried to remember the last time he'd said more than "uh-huh" or "you too" when someone said they loved him.

He hung up the phone immediately and spurred Bear toward the barn. All this emotional stuff was wearing on him, and he had enough pressure waiting for him at home. With an angelic face and the ability to make his entire body heat with a single touch.

Had Emery Reeder been sent by heaven so they could heal each other, or was she sent by Satan's henchmen to ferret out the secret and avenge her brother's death in the process?

Heck if he knew. Papa claimed he was smart, but he was just a simple rancher, and not a "super sexy rancher" like that shirt Maddie gave him claimed.

As he rode home, he smiled at the memory of Emery holding that shirt and teasing him about it.

He was seriously messed up right now.

Chapter Seven

Shafts of warm sunlight had Emery blinking against the brightness as consciousness returned. She was groggy and disoriented as if she'd only slept a few hours.

A comfortable mattress and pillow were beneath her, and the savory smell of bacon filled her nose and made her stomach growl.

She looked around an unfamiliar room and out large windows at a gorgeous lake with green mountains surrounding it. She tried to orient herself to her surroundings and why she was so exhausted. It took half a beat for it to connect where she was.

Greer Delta's guest bedroom.

Exhaustion fled and her stomach filled with a tingling that was either pleasant or unsettled. At the moment, she wasn't sure which. She scrambled upright in the bed and peered out the still open bedroom door. She could hear movement in the kitchen and could smell bacon and maybe something sweet cooking as well. It was impossible to see much more than the back of the gray leather couch and a big screen on the wall from this angle, but the man was definitely out there. Waiting for her. Making her breakfast.

All she needed was to cue the creepy music: na na na na, na na na na.

But ... Greer didn't seem like a creepy, sinister, disturbing, mean guy. Far from it. If only the incredible Greer who'd held her last night and was so tender and protective of her wasn't also the Growly Greer who had killed her only brother. She was in such a mess, muddle, chaos, confusion, predicament, disaster even. She wasn't sure if she should blame the Voice, Greer, or herself.

She plucked at the hem of her T-shirt that barely covered the important parts. Her eyes widened. It wasn't her T-shirt. She was wearing Greer's T-shirt.

Everything from last night played over again in her mind. It was surreal. She'd clung to Greer as if he were her deliverer. Well, maybe not as pure as that. She'd clung to him as if he was the most captivating cowboy of the century. He reminded her of ... Maverick. She loved that movie. Mel Gibson as a cowboy. The blue eyes and that smile of Greer's was ... yummy.

It felt strangely intimate to be wearing his T-shirt in the light of day. As if they were dating and she regularly wore his T-shirt to sleep in to keep him close to her heart.

Weird. Not good. But somehow alluring and forbidden and flirtatious and fun too. Yikes.

Sliding out of bed, she grabbed her backpack and was headed for the bathroom when she saw her shirt and shorts—washed, folded, and waiting for her on the floor by the open doorway. Another kind act from Growly Greer. Dang it, he kept stacking them up.

Did she dare grab her clothes? She was out of sorts and not ready to risk seeing Greer until she'd showered, dressed, done her hair and makeup, and most of all prayed hard. She needed to be at peak intellectual performance, full of spiritual insight, and looking her best to have the confidence to win this battle. A battle she wasn't even sure how to fight. Somehow she had to be Taylor Miles and avenge Travis, serve her country like her brother had done for years and had died trying to do.

She crept toward the bedroom door, her eyes fastened on the living area. As she got closer, she could see Greer with his back to her in the kitchen. He had the fridge open and looked to be grabbing something out of it. She hurriedly picked up the clothes and straightened.

He turned with a gallon of milk in his hand. His mouth dropped open slightly and he stared at her while holding the milk aloft. He stared like she was an angel straight from heaven.

With her backpack in one hand and her clean clothes in the other, she couldn't self-consciously pat down her mass of curls, straighten the T-shirt that had slipped off one shoulder when she bent down, or tug at the T-shirt to cover ... at least part of her legs. Greer must be more legs than upper body; for such a tall guy, his T-shirt wasn't nearly long enough on her.

Neither of them moved, and she wasn't sure she was breathing. She'd had a lot of men tell her she was beautiful or give her appreciative and sometimes leering looks. She'd never had a man look at her like this. His blue eyes were magnetic. Her stomach filled with warm bubbles, and she couldn't stop herself from smiling at him.

"Good morning, Maverick." Her voice was all breathless and far too telling.

"Maverick?" He gave her a hesitant smile, as if worried she'd lost her mind.

"You know, the sexy cowboy from the movie. I think Mel Gibson played him?" Think? She knew. She should stop talking now. Had she really said, "sexy cowboy?" Greer froze as if shocked as well. "I mean, you're kind of more Clint Eastwood with how serious and reticent you are, not nearly as flirtatious as Maverick, but I think I'll call you Maverick." She loved the idea of calling him something besides Growly Greer. If he was Maverick, he wasn't the guy who'd shot her brother. Right?

"Reticent?"

"You know, quiet, restrained, tight-lipped, withdrawn, uncommunicative, taciturn."

He chuckled, set the milk down, and rubbed at his stubbled jawline. "Maverick's okay," he said.

She bit at her lip. Maverick. Her sexy, kind, quiet cowboy who was protecting her from her fake boyfriend. Justin? Was that what she'd called the guy? She was writing her own script now. Emery loved books and movies far too much, but she'd never tried to put herself into the screenplay like this. As far as fantasy guys went, Greer or Maverick fit the bill pretty incredibly. He wasn't the suave or teasing hero, but he was tough, protective, ultra-handsome, and made her stomach hop happily.

What was happening? This wasn't some book or movie. This was her life, and this man was a dark-hearted killer. Her smile disappeared and she backed away, muttering, "I'm going to shower."

She glimpsed concern in his blue gaze, but she needed to break away right now. Slamming the bedroom door behind her, she didn't bother locking it. Greer had proven he could get through the lock, but more importantly she knew he'd never be the man to walk in while she showered. He'd come in last night, but that was because she'd been screaming her head off. She was sure his protective nature wouldn't allow him to sit idly by.

Hurrying through the shower and putting on her vanilla sugar body splash and what little makeup she'd brought, she felt almost human. She folded his T-shirt and set it by her makeup products and backpack in the bathroom, smiling at the saying on the front and remembering how fun it had been to tease Greer about it.

She'd had no idea what to expect coming here, and it had been horrifying to walk out of those trees and into the presence of her brother's murderer. She'd felt more comfortable and intrigued around Greer and in his house than she could've ever foreseen.

She kneeled and prayed for help, strength, protection, and most of all discernment. Seeing clearly had never been so crucial. She should've stayed on her knees and listened for some inspiration, but Greer was cooking that delicious-smelling breakfast. She was hungry, and she didn't want to keep him waiting.

She straightened, put on a smile, and walked through the bedroom, flinging the door wide and striding out into the main area. Greer was pacing the kitchen and turned at the sound of the door opening. Again, he stared at her. She paused and then flipped her long hair over her shoulder and asked, "What? Have you never had a girl stay in your house before?"

"Mom, sister, or cousins," he said.

"Oh." She walked bravely toward him. "So I should feel extraordinary dwelling where no unrelated woman has ever dared trod?"

His slow grin came, and he nodded.

Though he said nothing, his smile and his look were enough to light a fire inside of her. Emery had to look away. She glanced out his huge floor-to-ceiling windows and whistled. "Gorgeous doesn't even begin to describe that view."

He still said nothing, which she was beginning to see was normal for him. She looked back at him and cocked an eyebrow. "What? You see such beauty every day that it's become commonplace for you?"

His gaze slowly traveled over, and she'd never had a compliment so sincere bestowed upon her.

"No," he finally said.

"No what?" She would force this man to talk if it was the last thing she did. It was a quest now.

"I've never seen such beauty," he said, staring directly at her.

Emery gasped and put a hand to her neck, trying to remember to breathe. She hadn't meant to bait him like that. She could only guess this man didn't gush out compliments to anyone. She felt special, unique, elite, and exceptional. She wanted to hug him and kiss him. He boldly held her gaze, and she was in desperate trouble of forgetting who he was, who she was, and why she was here. Flirting with and getting Greet to talk wasn't the objective. Finding some military secret and avenging her brother was her purpose.

This was all getting completely out of control, so before she did anything she'd regret, she looked to the table set with dishes, syrup, butter, chunky peanut butter, and bowls with sliced strawberries, bananas, blueberries, and raspberries. "You made me breakfast?"

Instead of answering, he turned and pulled a cookie sheet out of the oven. It was loaded with plates of eggs, bacon, and pancakes. He walked over to the table and set it down in the middle. No hot pad or trivet on the table, so she'd guess it wasn't too hot. She loved how true Greer was to himself at all times. No fancy platters here. Basic white stoneware and a cookie sheet as the serving tray.

He pulled out a chair for her and gestured with his hand. The look on his face matched the feeling inside her. He was interested in her, but he was leery. Did that mean he knew she was Emery? A shiver slid down her spine at the thought. How could she find out without getting kicked out of his beautiful house?

Or worse, shot between the eyes.

She sank into the chair and gave him a wobbly smile. He nodded and hurried back to the kitchen, pulling milk and orange juice out of the fridge, then returning and setting them on the table. He must've put the milk back away earlier when he'd seen her in only that T-shirt. The fear disappeared and a delicious shiver trailed through her at the memory.

Greer sat kitty corner from her. As if he wanted to stay close but didn't want to sit directly across from her and stare at her throughout breakfast. Did he want to stay close because he liked her, or because he thought she'd go berserk and try to throw the butter knife at him?

The bacon smelled delicious, but her stomach was pitching all over the place with worry and she wasn't sure she could eat a thing.

Greer met her gaze and asked, "Prayer?"

She wasn't sure if he was asking if she was all right with prayer or if she would offer the prayer. Nothing about this man was lining up with her already ludicrous expectations of what he'd be like. Prayer, huh? She wanted to hear him say the prayer, hear him string together more than a few words in a sentence. She also wanted to know if he was a token Christian or a real one.

Would a real Christian murder her brother? No. But if he killed him completing what he thought was an assignment from higher ups, as a soldier, she supposed he could be forgiven. But he would be conflicted. Looking into Greer's eyes, she could see that he *was* conflicted. She'd thought it was because he knew she was Emery, but maybe it was something deeper than even that.

"I'd love to have a prayer over the food. Would you offer it, please?" She blinked at him, she hoped prettily. It was out of line for a guest to ask the host to offer the prayer, but what was one more strike against her at this point?

That must have surprised him, as he gave a grunt of surprise and a crooked smile. Then he shook his head and put his hand out.

Emery swallowed hard. Could she take his hand? Every time she'd touched him, it had messed with her mind. Last night had been bizarre, and she couldn't repeat the hugging and letting down her guard with him. But she'd said she'd pray with him and asked him to voice it. If she refused to hold his hand now, it would be all kinds of awkward. They had more sparks but also awkwardness going on between them than any of her junior high dance partners. She could picture her and Greer at those junior high dances. Her hands barely touching his shoulders. His hands pinching the waistline of her dress.

Two feet of distance between them as they shuffled back and forth and tried not to look at each other, but they wanted to look and they wanted to get closer.

Placing her hand in Greer's, she tried to distract herself by thinking of junior high dances, but she couldn't ignore the warm pulse that went through her as his fingers threaded with hers and their palms slid together. Just like those first touches from a boy that were all sparkle and tingles. There was nothing awkward about Greer holding her hand, and he was all man. If it was any other man in this world—well, any man close to her age without severe halitosis—she would've proposed marriage based on the connection of this hand-holding alone.

Emery quickly bowed her head and shut her eyes tight so he wouldn't see how affected she was. She didn't want to know if it affected him, too.

Greer cleared his throat and began, "Dear Father. We thank thee for the food, for all thou blesses us with. We thank thee Taylor is here. Please bless, protect, and lift her. Please bless the food. In the name of our Lord and Savior Jesus Christ. Amen."

"Amen," Emery echoed. She didn't move. She kept her head bowed and her hand in his. The spirit was strong in the room. Greer didn't waste words and it was a very formal prayer, especially for her underspoken cowboy. He'd officially talked more than she'd heard him speak previously. He'd been grateful she was here and asked for her to be blessed and protected. As Taylor. At least he believed the lie, but she wanted to hear his deep voice say her real name.

She forced herself to pull her hand back and look up. Greer offered her a shy, endearing smile. How could this man be a killer? Her brother's killer? Maybe he wasn't. Maybe the Voice had made it all up or gotten misinformation. She wanted to explore that possibility but feared she was grasping at excuses to like Greer.

Neither of them said anything as he waited for her to dish up, and then he got himself food while she piled fruit on her pancakes and drizzled them with the butter syrup. She poured herself some milk, put her napkin on her lap, and ate a bite of eggs. They were incredible. Buttery and cheesy, and was that sea salt?

"Yum," she declared. "These are the best eggs I've ever had."

"Thanks." He sounded as if the word had cost him a lot.

She ate a bite of the pancake and again was stunned. The berries and syrup and fluffy sweet pancake were better than a bakery-made pastry. "Wow. Do you always cook like this?"

He shrugged, then nodded.

Emery smiled. "Do you ever talk much?"

He shook his head, but the corners of his mouth turned up.

"So you live here desperately and forlornly alone, and you never converse with anyone, even your livestock or your favorite canine? Wait, do you have a dog? You simply must have a dog. A cowboy isn't complete without his faithful hound at his side." She ate a bite of bacon. Cooked perfectly. Not burned, but still crispy. And this was no cheap, fatty bacon. This was the good stuff that rich people had the butcher cut for them that was leaner than average but better tasting.

She'd earned a slightly larger smile. "Brave," he murmured.

"Your dog's name is Brave, or I'm brave to tease you?"

He actually laughed. She really loved his laugh. She needed to stop liking so many things about him, but if she was going to get his guard down and find out about the secret, she needed to act well the part.

"Brave's my dog."

"Why didn't he come greet me last night? Doesn't he ride the range with you?" She ate another bite of the buttery eggs.

He shook his head. "Too old."

"Ah, that's sad. Can I meet him after breakfast?"

"Sure."

"Thanks." She winked at him and focused on her breakfast. He seemed relieved to not be conversing as he ate. Slyly studying him while she enjoyed breakfast, she noticed he had good manners but ate rapidly like he was on a mission. She was stuffed full and only had a little food left on her plate. He'd refilled his and was still plowing through the bites.

Leaning back, she openly studied him. He stopped with a fork full of eggs halfway to his mouth. "You okay?" he asked.

She smiled. "Yes, thank you. The food was scrumptious. I'm ready to burst so I'm scrutinizing you while you partake."

He slowly lowered his fork back to his plate.

"No, no, no." She gestured with her hands. "Scoop it up. I'm in absolutely no rush. But can I ask some questions while you devour your victuals?"

He stared at her as if she'd lost her mind, but then he smiled. "Victuals," he muttered. Then he shook his head and went back to eating.

Most people would probably wonder what her questions were, but Greer was not most people. He didn't need to prove himself to anyone. He was simply confident in who he was and comfortable in his own skin. It made her feel comfortable around him. He also seemed to instinctively accept and not judge her. Which was insane if he knew she was Emery. She should be terrified of him, or at the very least be repelled by him for what he'd done. She was neither.

"So, first question," she said.

He nodded.

"Why the thee and thou in your prayers? Are you Amish?"

He chuckled and swallowed a drink of juice before saying, "Respect."

"Hmm." She regarded him. Every word mattered with this man. He did seem like the type to be very respectful of deity, elderly people, and positions of authority.

Suddenly clanging bells seemed to sound in her head. That was it. She'd wondered earlier, but that *had* to be why he'd killed Travis. Someone in authority had told him to, and though Greer was definitely independent and tough and responsible for himself, he also was the type to follow orders from authority or someone he respected. Did that make him less responsible for Travis's death or did it make him a mindless sheep who just followed his shepherd? Who was his shepherd? That's who Emery needed to go after. What if his shepherd told him to eliminate Emery? Her throat constricted.

Several beats passed as he ate and she tried to calm her racing heart. Finally, he looked up at her as if awaiting her next question. Emery forced herself to plunge ahead and try not to worry about someone telling Greer to shoot her in the head and him obeying. He'd promised to protect her and keep her safe. She clung to that.

"Are you in the military?" she asked.

"No."

His body seemed to tighten at the question. Sore spot? Hadn't the Voice said he wasn't military but was trained as a lethal weapon? She had to find out if the Voice could even be trusted. Everything he'd told her about Travis seemed to be true.

"Did you used to be in the military?"

He finished chewing his bite as he shook his head no. His blue gaze was intense, as if he didn't like her line of questioning.

"Have you been trained to fight and shoot a gun?"

His brows drew together. He plunged in another bite of pancake.

"Forgive me. That query feels too direct to you?"

He shrugged, not answering.

"O-kay. Mr. Mute doesn't want to answer."

His brows rose as he darted a glance at her.

"It's all right. I can keep asking my questions. I didn't mean to upset you; you just seem like a tough dude who could take care of business if necessary and you did pull a gun on me yesterday. Just

76

wondering who trained you to be like that or if it's just instinctive." She was talking too fast, still half afraid he would take care of business and eliminate her after he finished his bacon. The bright sun glittering off the mountain lake and the warm, accepting presence of Greer reassured her enough to not run screaming into the mountains.

"Not upset," he said, crunching on his final piece of bacon.

She waited, but that was all he was giving her. He was a tough nut to crack for sure. "Okay, a couple more questions. Then we'll go meet Brave and if you don't mind, I'd love an introduction to your horses."

He gave her his slow grin and a nod.

She really liked that grin. She rubbed her hands together, pushing her worries aside. Greer couldn't possibly hurt her. He was a true gentleman cowboy and the Voice had said he would respect and protect women.

"I'm so excited about the horses. Okay, last question for the breakfast table. Why do you eat like you're a fireman and there's going to be an emergency at any moment?"

He had his fork almost to his mouth with his last bite of pancakes, but he set it down at that question. His plate was almost clean. He'd probably been taught to "polish it clean" like Sister Weatherspoon had expected of Travis and Emery. Sometimes Emery left food on her plate simply because she wanted to be a bit rebellious, but over the past nine years she hadn't been able to afford that luxury.

Now with the money from the Voice, she supposed she could be wasteful. She had no idea what to do with all that money. Maybe after she got the location of the weapon and went back to teaching school, she could donate it to World Orphans, her favorite Christian charity.

"Busy," he muttered.

"I'm sure you're a very busy, very productive cowboy, but you should try to slow down and savor your food. That was the most delectable breakfast I've ever had, and I'm not sure you fully experienced the flavor of one delicious bite." She was teasing him, which should've been awkward as he didn't seem like a guy most people would even attempt to tease. He was the last person on earth she should want to tease with, but she found she couldn't help herself.

He smiled and shook his head. Then he lifted his fork that was loaded with pancake, peanut butter, bananas, and berries. He put it in his mouth and very slowly chewed, staring at her the entire time.

"Um ... yeah ... so delicious ... ooh, la la ... mmm-hmm," she murmured in a fake husky tone as he ate. "I'm just helping you to enjoy the full experience."

He swallowed his bite and chuckled at her. "Thanks." Drinking some milk, he asked with no prompting on her part, "Finished with questions?"

She was impressed. He was trying to continue the conversation. "Apologies, but I do have one more. Peanut butter on your pancakes?"

He nodded. "Delicious and nutritious."

She laughed. "I'll take your word for it. And look at all the words you're sharing with me. If you were one of my students, I'd give you a four."

"Four? Not an A?"

"Nope. No letter grades in elementary school, thank you very much. Four means proficient, competent, adept, skilled, capable. Hmm ... nope. Honestly, you haven't talked enough to deserve a four. Maybe a two and a half. I was being benevolent earlier."

He laughed again. Then he stood and started cleaning up breakfast. Emery stood to help. She would do about anything to make him laugh.

Even give up on your quest to avenge your brother?

She startled and got a sideways glance from Greer.

Anything but that. She had to think of Travis and be loyal to her flesh and blood. If the Voice was to be believed, she had to play her part, complete Travis's mission, and be a true patriot to her country. There was no need to hurt or imprison Greer. She could easily believe he was a warrior but a pawn. She didn't want any harm to come to him.

But Greer was proving to be much more than she'd bargained for. Already she found herself not hating him or thinking of him as "growly." She had to somehow keep her distance or she'd fail the mission and probably put herself in grave danger.

Chapter Eight

Greer was more impressed with, drawn to, and confused by Emery Reeder in the light of day than he had been last night when he'd still hoped she might be Taylor Miles. When he'd turned from grabbing milk out of the fridge and she'd been standing framed by the guest bedroom door wearing only his T-shirt, he about had heart failure. The shirt had slipped off one shoulder and only covered the tip-top of her thighs. The smooth, firm, tanned shoulder and legs he'd seen were more appealing than any model could be. At least to him.

It wasn't just physical beauty that Emery Reeder possessed. She had an inner light and warmth about her that took him by surprise. She was funny, intellectual, and could talk the hind legs off a mule. He loved it. He could listen to her talk all day, and he spent most of his days in silence. He hadn't realized how much he'd been missing out on. Listening to her talk, holding her hand while he prayed, savoring a bite of food at her instruction, laughing, seeing her smile. How on earth could this woman be the mercenary Travis Reeder's sister? It made no sense, and he wished he knew more about Travis and could somehow bridge the gap to Emery.

They walked out to the barn together into the bright sunny morning. July second. His family would have an enormous party on the fourth. Would he miss it this year to be with Emery? He didn't mind. He loved his family, but social events weren't his ideal way to spend his time.

He wanted so badly to hold Emery's hand as they walked. Or maybe he'd get brave enough to place his hand on the small of her back as he'd seen his brother Thor do with his fiancée Shelly. He shook his head to clear it. He was supposed to figure out why she was here, not fall in crush with her.

"You shouldering that heavy load all right over there, Maverick?"

He smiled. She had no idea how heavy his load was. Or maybe she did. He found himself wanting to tease with her, and he never wanted to tease with anyone. "Top Gun?"

"No-o," she drawled out, shaking her head. "I love Tom Cruise's smile, but you are the cowboy through and through. Do you like me calling you Maverick?"

"Sure." She could call him anything she wanted. His chest tightened. Unless she called him murderer. Oh, man. Hopefully Papa would figure out who had sent her here. Sweet, funny Emery must be misguided, probably by the same people who had paid her brother to resort to kidnapping and murder to find the Delta secret. Maybe Travis had been lied to as well.

If she knew he'd killed her brother, she had to hate him. How could she act this appealing, kind, and fun with him if she knew he'd killed Travis? What did he know? He was no expert on women. He'd failed with Belinda, the one woman he'd thought he was meant to be with. His cousins and sister were great, but he'd mostly stayed quiet and out of trouble by not rocking the boat with them. Unlike Chandler, Thor, or Hudson who teased them all nonstop. He swore they did it just to get a reaction.

Emery looked him over as they stopped next to the barn. "Or maybe I should call you Rooster."

"Rooster?"

"Goose's son. In the new movie?"

He shook his head. He'd never seen the new Top Gun, only the old one back in middle school, and it had been old then.

"Ah, you're missing out. We'll have to watch it together. Sooo good." She leaned against the barn and he'd never seen a more appealing sight. What would she do if he pinned her against the barn and kissed her? His face heated, and he tried to focus.

"Rooster was super cute," she continued, adorable and appealing as anyone he had ever seen. "He had this mustache ..." She drew in a breath. "Smoldering, blazing, glowing, *fiery* hot." She winked and Greer found himself jealous of some man named Rooster. "And he plays the piano and sings like Goose did in the first movie. 'This kind of love drives a man insane,'" she sang out. "'You broke my will, oh what a thrill, goodness, gracious, great balls of fire!'"

Greer laughed. He would surely set some kind of record for the most laughter out of his mouth in twenty-four hours.

"Would you grow your mustache longer and shave your beard for me if I begged you pretty please?"

Greer's eyes widened, and he scrubbed at his short beard. She blinked up at him so prettily he almost lost his mind. He'd grow a mustache for her. He wanted to ask if she'd kiss him if he begged *her* "pretty please."

Blinking quickly to clear his vision of what kissing her might be like, he opened the small man door and held it for her. They walked into the dim, cool interior of the barn. There was enough light from the skylights and the windows that he didn't bother with the light switch.

"Yay!" She clapped her hands. "I can't wait to meet all of your people."

Greer chuckled, shaking his head. They slowly walked around and he introduced her to Bear, Bruin, Beau, and Brooks, his horses, and then they found Brave napping in a corner. His dog looked up at them and Emery immediately squatted down to pet him. Brave moaned and leaned into her. Greer needed to find a new dog to help with the cattle, but it felt like a betrayal to replace Brave who'd been a gift from his dad for his twelfth birthday. He and Brave had grown up together.

"Ah, that's a good boy." Emery peered up at Greer, a twinkle in her dark eyes. His heart missed a beat, and it was all he could do to not rub at his chest. She was going to tease him, and he could hardly wait to hear what she had to say.

"So, what is *with* all the B names?" she asked.

His eyes widened and his gut suddenly churned. No way was he telling her about Belinda. He'd only talked to Esther and Papa about Belinda ditching him for her career as an exercise consultant and then meeting someone at the gym, someone who could "actually share their feelings with her instead of grunt" and telling Greer "goodbye forever".

Some of his siblings or cousins knew how in love he'd been with Belinda back in the day, but thankfully they never said anything or teased him. She'd been gone from the valley for over two years now, but when they'd dated she'd renamed his horses with B names like her and like Brave. He'd thought it was cute at the time. He hadn't renamed them after she left. Possibly hoping she'd come back?

He shrugged, saying nothing and having to resist the urge to fold his arms defensively across his chest.

Emery straightened and walked closer to him. It amazed him that she wasn't afraid of him. Had she come here on her own to discover what had happened to Travis? That wouldn't explain her having money to pay cash for everything. He had to think she didn't know who had killed Travis, or she wouldn't be so sweet with him. His heart ached for her. If only he could hold her and somehow make things right for her. But he couldn't. He couldn't bring her brother back.

She blinked up at him, those long lashes framing her dark eyes. She was so beautiful he wondered if staring at her would blind him like the sun.

"So ..." She tilted her head to the side of the garage where his John Deere 2025R was parked. "What's the tractor's name?"

"The tractor?"

"Yeah." She flipped her long hair all sassy and cute and sashayed over to the tractor. Greer watched her go. She must've been a dancer at some point because she moved in ways that shouldn't be legal. He was enthralled by her. She trailed her fingers along the tractor's body and Greer found himself jealous of an inanimate object. "Everybody else has their B name. This guy deserves one too."

He rubbed at his jaw. Did he explain the tractor wasn't alive? She grinned and of course he smiled back. What was a guy to do?

She walked slowly around the tractor and he simply stared at her. "Babe ... Bubbly ... Butterscotch ... Booboo ... Blondie ... Badger ... Beautiful ... Bambie?"

With each name, she shot him a look and he shook his head no, fighting laughter, but with Bambie he couldn't hold it in any longer. He busted up, and she laughed with him.

They sobered after a few incredible seconds and she kept going. "Belle ... Butterfly ... Bug ... Bean ... Bubbles ... Ballerina?"

His cheeks hurt from smiling so big. He'd let Belinda name his horses and dog, but even his fond memories of her before she'd walked out of his life didn't hold a candle to this moment.

"You have to say yes or no," Emery teased him.

"No."

"No Ballerina? Hmm." She patted the tractor. "I'm running out of ideas, girl."

"Girl?" His tractor was tough and impressive and a John Deere for crying out loud. His sister and cousins were tough, but still female. Yet he didn't think a tractor could be feminine.

At Emery's raised eyebrow and pointed look with that conspiratorial gleam in her dark eyes, he decided his tractor could be anything she wanted it to be. After all, his cousin Alivia was a beautiful lady but also tougher than most men.

"I thought you'd agree. She's a beau-ti-ful ... piece of equipment." Emery smirked at him and turned back to the tractor.

Greer could only think what a beautiful lady Emery was. If he'd been inclined to speak and wasn't such a conflicted mess over this woman, he might have told her so.

"Okay, sweetie." Emery walked around to the front of the tractor and faced it head on. "We've got to find a name for you. Bestie?"

Greer shrugged. It wasn't her worst name.

"No ... Boss." Emery nodded her head as if it was decided. She looked to Greer, and he found himself nodding. He liked it.

"You have to say yes or no," she teased him.

"Yes." He stared deeply into her eyes and the moment seemed to slow down.

Greer had no choice. He had to show her that he was a man who was gone over a woman. He would stride up to her, wrap her up tight, and kiss her until it was time for nightly chores, and it was only ten in the morning. He loved the idea.

His phone beeped in his pocket. Greer startled. He wasn't a texter any more than he was a talker.

"Excuse me," he murmured. He caught a glimpse of frustration on Emery's face as he turned away and glanced at the phone. Papa.

Are you away from the house? I saw you walk in the barn but never leave.

Crap. He was supposed to get Emery away from the house far

enough that Papa and Thor could sneak in and install those cameras. He wanted to tell them not to do it. He trusted her.

But that was stupid of him. There was no good-for-him reason that Travis Reeder's sister had lied her way into staying at his house and was being so irresistible that he wanted to fall for her. He'd stupidly trusted Belinda with his heart years ago and she'd left him because of her career. When she broke up with him, she'd admitted he was "emotionally closed off and unable to share his feelings or hold up his end of the conversation." What made him think Emery could ever care about a nonverbal cowboy like him, even if they didn't have the impossible obstacle of him having killed her brother? Dumb.

Give me ten, he texted back.

Ok.

He pocketed his phone and looked back at Emery. Brave had used the energy to stand up and walk to her side and she was scratching his head. She met Greer's gaze and his chest filled with warmth. How would he resist her? She had to be putting on an act, but his heart didn't want to believe it. He should text Papa back and tell him he couldn't do it. He could not be around this woman and stay detached and immune and figure out who had sent her here and protect the Delta secret. He was in extreme danger—the emotional kind.

"Horse ride?" he asked when he wanted to tell her the truth, get the truth out of her, and then kiss her for hours.

"Yay!" She clapped her hands together. "I thought I'd grow old and gray anticipating that delicious question."

He smiled. Delicious? She'd taste delicious when he kissed her. That was for sure. He shifted his hat lower over his eyes. He needed to get her out of here. Maybe exploring the picturesque trails south of the lake on horses would give him some space to calm down. He couldn't stare into her eyes if she was riding a horse on a trail that wasn't wide enough to ride side by side.

Turning, he walked to his tack closet and started pulling out bits and bridles. Movement came from behind him, and he glanced back to make sure she wasn't coming at him with a knife.

Of course she wasn't. Emery was smiling broadly as she sidled in next to him and bumped his shoulder with hers. "How can I help?"

Greer paused and could only stare at her. How could she help? She could stop being so perfectly intriguing and making his heart long for something that would never happen. He couldn't trust her as she might plunge a knife into his back, and he definitely couldn't fall for her and love her as he already longed to do after knowing her for less than twenty-four hours. She was Travis's sister. He could protect her like he'd promised because Greer always kept his promises.

He'd also promised to protect the secret. Would that put him in a quandary?

He handed over the halter, bit, and harness and then grabbed a pad and a saddle. They walked side by side over to Brooks, his most gentle horse.

"Pants," he muttered, sneaking a glance at her perfect legs.

She cocked her head. "Sorry, I'm all out of pants."

"You'll chafe."

She shrugged as if she didn't have a solution. He didn't have an ideal one either. He'd lay an extra blanket over her saddle and hope that helped.

"Have you ridden?" he asked.

She shook her head, gently stroking Brooks's mane as the horse came to greet them at the gate. "I'm a newbie. You'll have to teach me. I love to learn new things." For some reason, she trailed the tip of her tongue across her bottom lip and then grinned appealingly at him.

Greer went hot and cold all over. What was she doing with her lips? Did that mean she wanted to kiss him? Was he reading into everything she did and said? He kind of was, but who could blame him? There'd never been a womanly puzzle as intriguing and baffling as Emery Reeder. She was innocent and sexy at the same time. She was more incredible than any woman he'd ever met. And no way could he let down his guard and kiss her.

Please help me, he begged heaven above. Out of his element didn't begin to describe how messed up he was right now.

Chapter Nine

Emery's nether region was tender from riding a horse for over two hours. Greer had hurried to the house and come back with a soft blanket that he'd laid over the saddle before helping her onto the horse. She understood why cowboys and cowgirls always wore long pants and not shorts, but shorts were all she had. The blanket had helped her not chafe, thankfully, and she had absolutely loved the ride so far. Greer had led the way around the south side of the lake and then up some mountain trails. Brooks was obviously an older horse. He was gentle and obedient, and Emery thought he was perfect.

She didn't have to do much more than stay in the saddle as Brooks followed Bear, Greer's horse, along the trails. The mountains were exquisitely beautiful, green with thick undergrowth, pine and aspen trees, and the bright blue sky visible in pockets above the trees. It smelled like pine, cedar bark, and fresh air. She loved it here.

Unfortunately for her confused mind and heart, she loved the view of a tough cowboy seated so comfortably on his horse in front of her more than she loved the beauty of nature. Greer Delta. Wow.

He could ride a horse like nobody's business. He kept the pace slow for her, but it was obvious he'd been born to sit straight, tall, and perfect on his studly horse's back. Bear was a huge black stallion and he fit Greer. They could both star in any cowboy movie.

Too often throughout their ride, Greer would glance back at her and even under the shadow of his cowboy hat, she could see he knew she'd been staring. How could she help herself? He was far too good-looking, but more than that he was fun to tease, easy to talk to, strong and solid in all the ways that mattered. Greer seemed to be a man a woman could trust and love with every piece of her heart, body, and soul. She quivered just thinking about the times they'd touched and how he'd held her last night.

She should feel guilty that she was so taken by and impressed with the man who had supposedly killed her brother. She was starting to doubt the Voice. But that was wrong. Travis had believed in the Voice. She worried the Voice had wrong information or was deliberately misleading her and had done the same to her brother.

She had to ask the Voice more questions, but she felt almost afraid to. Why had she let herself be pushed into avenging her brother and helping her country with some dude whose name she didn't even know?

She hadn't had near enough time with Greer, but she appreciated what she knew. The only way he could've killed Travis was if Greer was completely deluded into thinking his family were the good guys and somebody had ordered him to kill Travis, thinking her brother was a bad guy. It was also possible Travis *and* the Voice were taking orders from the wrong side or had been misled.

She didn't know. She pushed away the confusion and the worries and breathed in the scent of pine and horse as she saw the lake come back into view. It was so gorgeous, blue and clear, and she could bet it was ice cold.

What could she do about her worries? If the Voice was the good guy, then she was doing what she should, getting Greer comfortable, getting to know him so she could find some secret weapon. If Greer was the good guy, then she was doing what she should, getting to know him and trust him so maybe someday she could confide in him who she was and what she was really doing here.

The problem with Greer being the good guy was it meant Travis was bad. No. Her brother had always loved and protected her. No matter how hardened the military had made him or what he'd gone through with his deployments, he'd been good on the inside. She favored the theory that Travis was the one tricked into thinking he was on the right side. He was a soldier and definitely would've obeyed orders.

That thought calmed her as they rode around the lake and made it back to Greer's barn with the sun high in the sky.

Greer swung off his horse and she should've followed suit, but it was so impressive how he moved that she found herself staring. He held on to Bear's reins and walked over to her and Brooks. He tilted his head back and she got a glimpse of those brilliantly blue eyes from underneath his cowboy hat.

"Reins," he said simply.

"Oh. You want these reins?" She flipped them in her hand.

He smiled and nodded at her.

She pulled the leather strap over Brooks's head and placed both ends in Greer's outstretched hand. He held onto the reins of both horses and walked the short distance to the barn door, looping the reins through the handle. Then he came to the left side of her horse and reached up for her. Of course he said nothing, but Emery didn't mind. She loved the silence and majestic beauty of this place, and if she could admit it to herself, of this man. Most of her days were spent with over twenty ten-year-olds all trying to get her attention and tell her stories. She adored her little people, but silence was bliss.

She pulled her right shoe out of the stirrup and swung it over the horse. Leaning forward, she put both hands on his broad shoulders as his palms wrapped around her waist. She pulled her left foot out of the stirrup and Greer easily lifted her to the ground.

Her legs almost collapsed out from under her. She wasn't sure if it was so much time in the saddle or how incredible it felt to have Greer's hands on her waist and him looking deeply into her eyes.

"Whoa!" she exclaimed. "I've got no horse legs."

He chuckled and held her up. Emery leaned into him, clinging to his muscular shoulders and amazed at how comfortable she was with him. He was so confident and secure with himself it seemed impossible not to relax and trust this stalwart, beautiful, steady man.

His smile slid away as he studied her. Really studied her. Like a man who was about to kiss a woman long and deep and thoroughly. She logically should not kiss him until she had some answers and knew who she could trust, but logic wasn't much help as Greer leaned closer and his warm palms pulled her tighter to his broad, lovely chest.

Bear nickered and then tossed his head impatiently. Brooks shifted, seeming almost annoyed as well.

Greer straightened and stepped away from her.

"Distracted," he muttered. Then he loosened the strap around each horse's belly and they both seemed to calm down.

Distracted? By her? Was that a good thing or a bad thing?

"Your legs okay?" he asked, inclining his head to her.

"They're fine," she lied. Her legs were shaky from being on the horse and her inner thighs were a little red despite the blanket, but she'd be fine. She didn't want him to worry or think she was a wimp. She wanted to be a tough cowgirl. This was the life.

Greer opened the large barn door, led the horses inside, and she tried to help him take all the gear off, offer the horses water and hay, and then brush them down. She probably wasn't much help, but she enjoyed being with him and Greer was patient as he showed her what to do and helped her. He didn't say much, but she didn't expect him to.

After they finished taking care of the horses they went inside, washed up, and constructed ham and turkey sandwiches with cut veggies for lunch.

She prayed and then started eating, surprised that she was even hungry after that huge breakfast and not working out today, though her rear believed that horse ride was quite the workout.

"Do you like teaching school?" Greer surprised her with not only a long sentence for him but initiating a conversation.

"Oh, yeah. My kiddos are the best."

He nodded as if encouraging her to tell him more, so she did. She told him about going to college on scholarship and working as a janitor and then getting her job. She told him all the things she loved about teaching grade school and some things she didn't. She told him funny stories about her kiddos and all the hilarious things they did and said. Everything she told him was the truth, except she said nothing about exactly where she'd attended college or where she lived or taught school. As it was Greer, he didn't ask, and she was grateful. She didn't want to lie to him.

Throughout lunch, she teased him about slowing down and "savoring" the delectable sandwich. He'd smile or occasionally even laugh. She wanted to make him smile and laugh more.

After they cleaned up lunch, she wasn't sure what they'd do. She finished wiping the table, rinsed the rag, and turned to him. He looked irresistible with his hair mussed and no cowboy hat on, in a T-shirt, jeans, and socks. He leaned against the counter with one hip and studied her. She could imagine he was as puzzled by her as she was by him. If he thought it was odd to have a houseguest with a supposed demented ex after her who was staying in his good graces and for an interminable amount of time, he didn't say anything about it or make her uncomfortable at all.

"So what do we do now?" she asked

What did cowboys do with their days? She assumed they were busy and worked hard, at least if Greer's body and the immaculate state of his house, barn, and corrals was any indicator, but what would the two of them do?

He smiled and straightened. "You can rest."

"No way. I will not rest while you work. I'm not some pampered girl who can't get dirty."

His gaze trailed over her, and she was suddenly hot from head to toe. Greer's slow smile grew and had her panting for air. Then he tilted his head toward the mud room.

She punched a fist in the air and danced around. "That's right. You recognize how hard-working I am and you know you will accomplish a myriad of tasks with your highly qualified and vastly experienced elementary school teacher by your side."

He let out a bark of a laugh.

"Was that a guffaw?" she demanded, her jaw dropping as she jutted one hip out. "Oh, don't you mess with me, Maverick. I will work you under your tractor. Or excuse me, under Boss."

He smiled, turned, and gestured toward the mud room.

She led the way, making sure she put an extra swing into her hips. She didn't worry about some objective. She didn't let herself think about Travis. She could only think about Greer.

When he let out a soft groan as she walked in front of him, she smiled to herself. It might be wrong of her and the complete opposite of what the Voice wanted, but she would get to know this man and enjoy this time with him. That was really the only way to complete her objective or find out who to trust, anyway.

Who knew Greer Delta would be the one who could heat her up with one glance and without one word? He was a brainteaser for her. She really, really liked brainteasers.

Chapter Ten

Greer could hardly believe how pleasantly the day had passed. Even harder to wrap his mind around was how perfect Emery Reeder was.

They weeded his garden and flower beds, mucked out stalls, and put fresh wood shavings down in the barn. They took a break and went on a ride on the lake in his kayaks. She made him smile and even laugh as she exclaimed over how cold the water was and kept begging him not to tip her over or splash her. Of course he said nothing and did neither, but he thought she was hilarious.

That night, they made dinner together. He had leftover steak from last night. He'd grilled a large pack and planned to use the extra meat in something. They made steak fajitas that were delicious, or in Emery's words, "delectable, appetizing, scrumptious, and mouthwatering." She teased him about slowing down and savoring the taste. He tried. He mostly savored being with her.

They headed back out into the perfect summer evening to do the night feeding and administer the medicine to the cows in the sick herd. Emery talked him into a short walk around the south side of the lake, asking him about his family. He told her each member of his family's name and thought that would suffice. Nope. Not for Emery. She wanted to know ages, what they did for work, where they lived, what their personalities were like, and what his favorite memory was of each one of them, cousins and all.

He talked more in that half-hour walk than he had in years. Crazily enough … it didn't kill him and he might have even enjoyed it. At least he enjoyed Emery being so interested in him and his family. Her ex-boyfriend didn't come up, and neither did anything that might point to her not being Taylor. Frankly, he was happy to avoid the whole topic.

But there was a warning bell clanging somewhere in his mind. If she was after the secret, of course she'd want to draw him out about his family and gain his trust.

He pushed that away and focused on Emery's long, dark hair curling down her back and swishing with each step she took. The setting sun sparkled along the east shoreline of the lake, but Emery's dark eyes sparkled more. He wished he could take her hand, but didn't feel he had that right.

After they washed up, she talked him into watching the old cowboy show Maverick with Mel Gibson. He'd seen it before, but they laughed a lot throughout. He was nothing like the smiling, charming Maverick on the show, but he wouldn't complain about being compared to Mel Gibson. His only regret was there was almost half a foot between the two of them on the couch during the movie. He would've loved to ease close and cuddle her against his side while he watched, but logically knew he should keep his distance from Travis Reeder's sister.

They stood and stretched after the movie. She inclined her head and gave him an appealing grin as the lights from the television lit her face. "Goodnight, Maverick."

"Night," he said in a weird, husky voice. He wanted to clear his throat but was afraid it would be too telling.

Her smile got bigger, and she turned and sashayed into her room. She shut the door behind her, but she didn't click the lock. What did that mean? Last night, the door had been locked and he'd had to pick it when she had the nightmare. Then after he held her, she'd pulled away and said her funny line about letting her scream and it was good for her vocal cords. She couldn't really mean that, but she'd seemed scared of him last night. He'd been certain that she knew exactly what he'd done. After spending the day together today, he could sense she'd grown comfortable with him and he thought she trusted him.

He groaned and pushed a hand through his hair. Turning, he strode into his own room and got ready for bed, but even after a very lengthy prayer, he had no answers and couldn't settle down and sleep.

Then he heard her screaming, "Travis, stop! No! Stop!" at the top of her lungs.

He was instantly out of his bed and running, grateful he'd slept in a T-shirt and shorts again just in case. Hurrying through the main area, his phone beeped on the dresser back in his room to warn him that there was movement in the main area. He hoped he wouldn't wake Papa with a notification. Papa could look in the cameras and see it was him if it did wake him up.

He stopped next to her door. Should he burst in there like he had last night? He didn't want to scare her again.

"Help! Stop! No!"

That made the decision for him.

Twisting the knob, he was grateful she hadn't locked the door so he didn't have to waste the time breaking in or feel guilty that he was picking the lock.

She was twisted in the sheets, and his eyes were adjusted enough to the darkness to see she was only in his T-shirt again. Emery in his shirt and sleeping in his guest room did funny things to his stomach, but he couldn't dwell on that. He had to rescue her from whatever violent dream she was having.

"No!" she screamed again, her voice hoarse.

Greer couldn't handle her being afraid. She'd been through enough being raised in foster care, losing her brother violently, and being brave enough to walk through the mountains straight to the man she should fear and loathe.

Maybe he was insane. He had no idea what twisted assumptions or instructions had brought her here, but he could remember asking Papa what he could do for Travis Reeder's sister. Papa had said all he could do was pray. He would keep praying, but now Emery was here with him, and he could take care of her and protect her, try to ease her pain.

"Em ..."

Wait—he couldn't call her Emery and force her hand. He wanted her to admit to him who she was. At that point, though, he'd have to admit to her face what he'd done. So maybe he wanted to keep her as Taylor for a good, long time.

"Taylor," he tried again, resting his hand on her shoulder.

"Help!" she screamed.

He sat on the bed next to her, wrapped his arms around her back, and lifted her off the mattress and against his chest. She was trembling and her face was scrunched up as if she were in pain. He wanted to stop her pain.

"Taylor," he tried again.

Her eyelids fluttered open. For half a beat she looked confused, and then she melted against him. "Ah, Greer. Thank you."

Her arms came around his lower back and she cuddled against him. Greer closed his eyes and rested his cheek against her soft curls, savoring this moment like she'd tried to get him to savor every meal they'd eaten today. He smiled to himself. He could definitely savor holding her.

She pulled back slightly and blinked up at him. Greer's breath caught. Was this the moment to kiss her?

He started leaning toward her, but there was something in her gaze.

She was afraid. Of him?

He stopped and asked, "You okay?"

She bit at her lip and shook her head. "I don't know. I've had this same nightmare every night since ..." Her eyes widened and she ducked out of his arms, scrambled the opposite way across the bed, and stood.

Greer stood as well, turning to face her, the mattress a barrier between them.

"Sorry," was all he could think to say.

"Not your ..." She stopped and then she stared at him.

Greer was almost certain she was going to say it wasn't his fault, but she'd been screaming her brother's name. If she knew Greer had killed him, then she couldn't really say it wasn't his fault, could she?

He'd chased down and killed bears, wolves, and coyotes who were killing his calves and cows. He'd been trained to fight and protect his family by his Papa and his dad and uncle, the best fighters he'd ever known. Greer thought of himself as brave, but at this moment ... he was a wimp. He should try to talk this out with her and tell her what had happened from his perspective and beg her to someday forgive him.

But he couldn't do it. So he turned and walked toward the bedroom door.

"Greer." His name was beautiful on her sweet lips.

He turned back. "Yeah?"

"Thank you for waking me up from my nightmare. I know I said I want to give my vocal cords a workout, but ..." She bit at her lip again and he barely held his ground. He longed to run toward her and pull her close. "I hate the nightmare."

He wished he was some verbose guy who could ask her about the nightmare and help her through all of this, but it was pretty twisted. He'd caused her nightmare in the first place, and now she was thanking him for waking her up from it.

Instead of saying anything, he tilted his chin to her and walked out, shutting the door behind him. He walked back to his room, responded to Papa's phone call with a text of, *Everything's okay*, then leaned against his wall and banged his head back against it. Everything was so far from okay. How could he be falling for Emery Reeder? At the same time, how could he not? He'd never met such an incredible and appealing woman.

He groaned and sank to his knees. Prayer was the only answer he had right now. Not just for himself, but for Emery.

Chapter Eleven

After a lot of desperate, rambling prayers, Emery finally fell back asleep. She thought she'd be more upset and terrified, but she focused on how incredible it had felt to be cocooned in Greer's arms and she felt at peace.

The next morning, she worried things would be tense and awkward between them, but again she felt surprisingly comfortable around him. Greer was kind and patient as ever. He'd already done the morning chores before she woke up and had sausage and French toast ready for her. She teased him about slowing down and savoring the food and he gave her the most irresistible smiles and sometimes even laughed.

A week went by. A crazy fast, incredible week. They fell into a comfortable but often exhilarating and confusing existence. Greer taught her things she could do to help him with different chores, unless it was something too intricate like when he rewired the barn's generator that had shorted out and she oohed and ahhed over how handy he was, to which she received a slow, embarrassed grin. Or something that required brawny muscle like lifting hay or straw bales and then she oohed and ahhed over how buff he was, to which she got a slow, adorable grin.

They took breaks from work occasionally and did some fun activities like kayaking, hiking, and mountain biking. He even took her rock climbing and rappelling, which terrified her, but she trusted Greer. That should've been the terrifying thing, how much she trusted him, but it was instinctive for her. She wanted to spend every minute with him.

On the Fourth of July, they'd had a private barbecue and watched the fireworks his family set off across the lake from his comfy back patio furniture. She felt bad he wasn't with his family because of her, but she was terrified to open up the can of worms that she wasn't Taylor, there was no boyfriend chasing her, that he should mistrust her and she should hate him. So she didn't broach the subject. He must've told his family not to come visit as no one bothered them, but she said nothing about it.

On Sunday they did only the basic chores, had a Bible study together, watched a few episodes of The Chosen, went on two long walks, and cooked more intricate meals.

She talked his ear off most of the time and often made him smile and laugh. Sometimes she got him to talk about himself and sometimes they had a comfortable silence between them.

She used his washing machine every night to wash her dirty clothes, socks, and underwear, then traded them out each morning. Every night she still slept in his T-shirt. He never said anything about her clothes.

In the late evenings, they went for a walk after nightly chores and then watched a movie. They didn't touch each other often, only when he helped her off a horse or when he held her each night after he woke her up from the nightmare. She wished the stupid nightmare would go away, but she loved having Greer hold her. It was not only comforting and sweet, but it made her warm all over and made her want to kiss him good and long. The problem was after the nightmare she was always reminded of why she was here and why she shouldn't be clinging to Greer, dreaming of kissing Greer, or letting herself fall for Greer.

This was Growly Greer, who'd murdered her brother.

But it wasn't. It was her cowboy Maverick.

He was her protector, her friend, and he made her heart race in a very pleasant way. She loved his smile, his patience, his tough body, his accepting nature, his handsome face, his confidence, his laugh, and his kindness to her. There wasn't much she didn't love about Greer.

Except that he'd killed her brother.

But had he? More and more, she was convinced that Greer could not have done it. The Greer she was coming to know and ... like very strongly, could never coldly shoot someone between the eyes. Especially a good someone like her older brother.

Could the Voice be lying to her, manipulating her to steal something from the Delta family? It seemed likely. The Voice texted her every night, hoping for updates and checking that she felt safe and comfortable. His texts came across as kind and patient. She kept telling him she was gaining Greer's trust like he'd asked her to and it wouldn't be an easy or quick thing. She also reassured him that Greer was a complete gentleman.

She wanted to call out the Voice and demand the truth, but she doubted he'd give it to her. She was tempted to tell Greer everything and see what he knew, what his perspective was, and if anyone in heaven loved her, he would tell her he absolutely hadn't killed her brother and the Voice was a liar and a con artist.

Did she dare ask?

Greer didn't say much, so it wasn't like he said her name often. But when he did, he called her Taylor. She wanted to hear Emery on his lips, right after he kissed her.

It was Wednesday night, eight days after she'd first arrived. They were trying to decide which movie to watch—she was lobbying for the old Top Gun—when the doorbell rang. They both froze. He'd told her that his family rarely came to see him. She looked at him and whispered, "Should I hide?"

He nodded.

She hurried into her bedroom and softly closed the door then leaned against it, trying to listen. She heard footsteps, followed by the door opening. A voice called out, "Greer! I'm here!"

"Hi, Bentley," Greer's deep voice came.

Bentley? Bentley? He didn't have a brother or cousin named Bentley, did he?

Their footsteps returned and she could hear this Bentley excitedly talking about a lacrosse game and Chandler. Greer did have a brother Chandler who played professional lacrosse.

There was a rap on her door. "Taylor?"

Her heartbeat ramped up. Who was this Bentley and what would him coming here tonight mean for her?

She pulled the door open and met Greer's blue gaze. He nodded to her and stepped back, revealing a thirty-something man who smiled pleasantly at her. There was something vacant about his gaze.

"Bentley," Greer said, "this is my ... friend."

Was he going to get away with not sharing her name?

"Hi, friend!" Bentley almost yelled. "You're pretty. You watch lacrosse with us?"

Emery looked from Bentley to Greer. He gave her an encouraging nod.

"I'd love to," she said.

"Chandler's game is on *right* now," Bentley informed her, hurrying over to plop down on the leather wraparound sofa.

Greer studied her as if discerning if she was all right. She smiled to reassure him, though she worried who Bentley would tell about a woman being at Greer's house. From all she'd come to learn about Greer this week, he wasn't a womanizer. She didn't know if he'd ever had a girlfriend. It would definitely stun his family to know a woman was with him.

"Come on," Bentley begged. "Turn it on." He patted the cushion next to him. "Sit by me, pretty friend."

Emery smiled. It didn't appear Bentley was dangerous. She and Greer turned toward the couch and Greer put his hand on her lower back. She startled as warmth spread through her. He was choosing to touch her, and she wasn't about to complain. He walked her to the couch, and she sat by Bentley. Greer settled on her other side. He turned on the game and Bentley started talking. He pointed out Chandler, number eighty-three. He explained rules to her when needed, cheered almost nonstop, usually happy cheers, but sometimes groaning if Chandler and his teammates weren't possessing the ball like Bentley wanted. At halftime, he demanded popcorn and drinks.

Greer gestured for her to stay seated, then made the popcorn and brought them all drinks. Bentley chatted with her about snow skiing throughout the break. Apparently he was the fastest skier in the valley.

Emery hadn't seen lacrosse before and she really enjoyed the fast-paced game, especially with Greer's brother being such a superstar and involved in a lot of the action. She also enjoyed Bentley. He was friendly, childlike, loud, and fun. It warmed her heart how much he seemed to love Greer and how good Greer was to him.

It hit her how welcoming and nonjudgmental Greer was. She'd felt nothing but kindness from him and obviously Bentley felt the same. It shocked her that his family and other friends didn't come by regularly simply to soak up the peace that was Greer Delta. She could almost bet he'd warned them all away because she was here.

It was in the fourth quarter when Bentley pushed her against Greer and said, "I thought you *friends*. You should hug."

Emery flushed from embarrassment but also from the length of Greer's firm body suddenly pressing against her. She didn't know how he'd react, but he shocked her completely when he slid his arm around her shoulders and drew her closer.

She gasped in surprise and felt Greer stiffen.

"Sorry," he murmured as he started to release her.

"Greer Delta," she whispered fiercely into his ear. "You let me go and I'll fracture your arm."

Greer chuckled in surprise. He stared down at her and asked, "You're okay?"

"Better than okay. Surpassing okay by miles." She tucked her feet up underneath her and leaned into him. Her right arm was trapped, but she slid her left hand across his taut abdomen and rested it on the firm muscles of his chest.

He sucked in a breath and his blue eyes were full of her as she glanced up at him.

"You're okay?" she asked.

He only nodded, but his gaze was warm and his touch was even warmer.

"And Chandler gets another assist!" Bentley screamed over the commentators. They refocused on the game in time to see the replay of Chandler passing the ball quickly to a teammate who popped it into the goal.

"He's the best!" Bentley crowed.

The rest of the game was a blur to Emery. All she could focus on was the pressure of Greer's arm around her, his warm palm on her upper arm, their bodies pressed together, and her hand touching his chest. Crazy that they'd been alone for over a week and their most intimate moment, besides after her nightmares, came when his friend was sitting on her other side cheering raucously for the lacrosse game.

As soon as the game finished, Bentley jumped up and said, "You drive me home?"

"How did you get here?" Emery asked.

"My brother, Jace. Good guy. Almost skis as fast as me. Like Greer. Good guy." He lowered his voice. "But Greer *not* the best skier."

Emery laughed.

Greer smiled down at her. "I'm not," he admitted.

Emery stared at him and whispered, "Don't tell Bentley, but I couldn't care less about your skiing abilities. You have many, many more important qualities."

He grinned. Their faces were so close they could've leaned in a fraction and kissed. She wanted to kiss him. He was a good guy. A great guy. The best she'd ever known. Knowing that this innocent man, Bentley, shared her opinion of Greer being a good guy not only warmed her heart but reassured her. This man could not have killed her brother.

She had to figure out why the Voice had sent her here and what this all-important secret was that had men lying and killing for it.

Did she dare confide in Greer and get his side of the story? Was it time for that? Or was it time to kiss him good and long and go from there? Her body trembled at the vision of that moment.

"Do you want to ride with us to my home?" Bentley asked from above them.

Emery looked up and he was right close, leaning over the back of the couch. She wanted to be with Greer, but this might be the only opportunity she'd get to snoop around and see if there was anything she could find about the Delta family secret. Knowledge was power, and she needed power over the Voice to figure out what his agenda really was.

Trust was also extremely important. She wanted to trust Greer. She also wanted him to trust her.

"Sure," she said, surprised by how easily she'd given up the opportunity to be alone and snoop.

Greer smiled as if her answer was the perfect one and she didn't even care about the missed opportunity. He stood, took her hand, and helped her up. He held on to her hand as they all walked through the house and into his garage.

"Tesla, Tesla!" Bentley cheered.

Greer looked at her, and she nodded. They hadn't driven anything out of his garage, sticking with the horses or walking or mountain biking. "I'd love to see my hot cowboy Maverick driving a sissy car," she teased, batting her eyelashes.

Greer grunted, but he was smiling. There was a depth to his gaze that thrilled her all the way through. She'd just called him *her* hot cowboy. They'd snuggled through part of a sporting event. She was trusting him instead of staying at his house and searching for the secret. Was tonight the right time to tell him all her secrets, to trust him completely?

"Who's Maverick?" Bentley asked.

"Me," Greer said, giving Emery his slow grin that made her stomach flip and her knees weak. Yep, she was kissing him tonight, and then someday soon she would tell him everything and trust that he could help her if the Voice really was a nefarious villain who'd tricked her brother and was trying to trick her. Of course Travis was still the heroic military man, but something was very wrong with the story and mission she'd been given.

Bentley shook his head. "You're Greer, silly." Bentley slid into the backseat. "Friend! You sit up front with Greer ... Maverick," he said in disgust. "That's a stupid name for my Greer." He slammed the car door.

Laughter spilled out of Emery. Greer chuckled and then he was laughing too. He wrapped his arm around her and walked her around the car. Emery felt like she was floating. None of the worries that had brought her here mattered at this moment. What mattered was she'd been led to Greer. It wasn't possible that Greer could've killed Travis, that he could be her enemy. Thinking her cowboy could coldly shoot somebody in the head was like saying gravity didn't exist and a person could float if they wanted to. It just didn't fit.

He leaned down close before he opened her door and his beard brushed against her cheek. It was soft and he smelled so good. She leaned into him.

"Let's go!" Bentley hollered from inside the car.

Emery laughed again. Greer opened her door, but before she slid in she whispered, "Thanks, Maverick."

He smiled and nodded to her. "Friend."

She grinned back.

The ride to Bentley's house on the northeast side of Summit Valley by a ski resort went quickly in the punchy Tesla. Bentley loved when Greer pressed on the gas and he chattered nonstop about Chandler and lacrosse the rest of the time.

When they got to his two-story cabin-style house, he jumped out and yelled, "Thanks, Greer! Bye pretty friend!"

"Bye," Emery said.

He slammed the door and darted toward the wide porch.

Greer glanced over at her and gave her a smile that made her quiver. He didn't say anything, but he took her hand, threaded their fingers together, and then placed their joined hands on his muscular thigh. Emery's quivers turned to trembles.

He drove quickly away from Bentley's house through the east side of the larger Summit Valley and then through the canyon back to his valley. Neither of them said a word, but the anticipation filling the car was palpable. Her stomach was dancing. Greer gently ran his thumb along the back of her hand and just that slight movement calmed her.

He parked in his garage and strode around to get her door. As he helped her out, it registered as always how handsome he was, but Greer was so much more to her than his good looks. He was the most patient, intriguing, and tough man she'd ever known. He was fun for her to be around. Though he didn't say much, he made her feel like every word out of her mouth was important and often funny. She loved the way she felt around him. She loved the way she felt close to him.

He held her hand as they walked through the garage and mud room and then through the main area. They stopped next to her open bedroom door. Emery smiled up at him, anticipation making her almost jumpy. She longed to kiss him. There were no lingering doubts. Greer was her protective cowboy, and he'd never do her wrong.

He released her hand and tenderly cupped her jawline with both of his large palms. His fingers threaded into her hair and his touch and the meaningful look in his blue eyes made her quiver.

Leaning close, he murmured, "Friend?"

Emery reached up and clung to his nicely formed biceps with both hands. "What can I do for you, my handsome Maverick?"

He smiled. "Can I kiss you?"

Emery trembled from head to toe. She trailed her tongue along her top lip and loved when he groaned softly. "If you don't kiss me, I'll tell the world the hottest, toughest cowboy I've ever met drives a sissy Tesla," she threatened. "And wears pink underpants."

Greer chuckled and then he softly, tantalizingly pressed his lips to hers.

Now Emery was the one groaning. The pressure of his kiss was perfect, and tingles erupted on her sensitive lips. She returned the pressure and clung to him as they tentatively explored each other's mouths in a sweet expression that wasn't demanding or in any kind of rush. Despite how tender it was, the passion in his kiss and his strong body pressed close almost overwhelmed her.

Emery ran her hands up his arms, over his shoulders and around his neck, tugging him ever closer. Greer slid his hands into her hair, gently massaging her scalp and making her tingle. He tilted her head slightly and continued to kiss her so beautifully. Of course it was perfect. This was Greer. She'd gone from terrified of this man and thinking she should hate him to wanting to spend every minute with him and thinking she may very well love him. Greer Delta was the perfect fit for her mouth and body. Could he be the perfect fit for her heart and soul?

He took the kiss to dizzying levels for a wonderfully long time. Then he eased back and studied her. His blue eyes seemed to penetrate her very soul. Did he already know her secrets? Would he hate her when she told him she'd crazily believed he killed her brother?

No. Not her Greer. He'd understand, he'd listen, and he'd help her and his family stay safe from the Voice or whoever their enemy was. Maybe he knew who had really killed poor Travis. Maybe he'd share whatever secret weapon his family was protecting.

Right now, she didn't care. She only wanted to focus on Greer and savor every moment. She blinked up at him, unsteady and so affected by him. She wanted him to lean back in and kiss her more. A lot more.

Instead he murmured, "Night," and sadly, woefully, regrettably, tragically released her.

She leaned back against the wall. "Goodnight, Maverick, Greer, my hot cowboy."

He smiled, but she could tell he was slightly embarrassed by her calling him hot. He was so perfect.

She wanted to fling herself at him, but he'd said goodnight. Greer was a righteous man. He probably wanted to make sure they didn't kiss too intimately, being all alone here. She staggered into her bedroom, not bothering to shut the door. Greer would come hold her after she had the nightmare as he did each night. This time, she would not let him go. She would kiss him again and then maybe she could finally tell him everything.

The kissing was all that really mattered at the moment. She put a finger to her lips and then she giggled like a teenager after her first kiss.

Greer Delta. What a man. Her man.

Really? Her man?

She wouldn't complain if the title could be true.

Chapter Twelve

Greer was in a hazy fog of beautiful feelings he'd never experienced as he walked on shaky legs from Emery's bedroom doorway across the main area and into his master bedroom.

He'd kissed her. He'd *really* kissed her. And she'd kissed him back. She'd clung to him and kissed him as if he were her missing piece.

Emery Reeder was the most intriguing, innocent, and wonderful woman in the world. Greer absolutely loved his mom, aunt, sister, and female cousins. They were the only women he could think of that came close to as incredible as Emery.

He walked into his bathroom, splashed water on his face, and brushed his teeth. His mind was on a constant repeat of those insanely wonderful kisses. He wanted to spout out poetry or something. He wanted to sing her his favorite country songs. She'd teased him about country music, but she hadn't complained when it had played on the radio.

Ah, Emery.

He changed into a T-shirt and shorts and paced his master suite. He had so much extra energy he wanted to go free climb up a cliff.

Emery.

He wanted to kiss her again and then say her real name. He'd hoped these past eight days that she would confide in him why she'd come, why she'd made up a cover story, who had given her information and paid her, and then he could tell her his side of the story with Travis. He ached to beg her to forgive him and hoped they could then start the path to healing together.

It still hurt him, deep in his soul, that he'd taken Travis's life. At the same time, he knew Papa and everyone else was right and he'd had to do it to protect Alivia and Klein.

Maybe the good Lord had orchestrated all of this like he'd felt so deeply the day Emery had first walked out of those trees. Maybe even the tragedy of Travis becoming a mercenary and his death could somehow come full circle and turn to something good.

Emery had come to him. She was better than good. She was incredible.

He'd gotten into the habit each night of not falling asleep until after Emery had the nightmare. She usually had it pretty early, around eleven. So intriguing, but sometimes disturbing, how the subconscious mind worked. He wished he could help her stop having the nightmare. Usually he held her after waking her up, but she always backed away. It must've been because the nightmare reminded her of Travis. That was okay. He'd keep holding her and helping her and showing her love until they both healed.

His phone beeped a text. Papa. His eyes widened. Papa had cameras in the main area. He knew his grandpa wouldn't be creepily watching them, but he might've glanced at the cameras and seen how close they were getting. What if he'd glimpsed that kiss? Greer's neck heated.

Can you call me?

Greer pushed out a breath, brushed his hand through his hair, and hit the button to call him. He hated talking on the phone worse than he hated talking in person. He hurried into his master bath and shut the door to muffle the sound if Emery was still awake.

"You all right?" Papa asked.

"Why?" Greer was surprised how demanding his voice came out.

"Just checking in, as you've sent no updates." Papa wasn't surprised by that, obviously. "Has she revealed anything about who hired Travis or who told her to come find you?"

Greer let out a breath. Papa hadn't seen him kiss Emery. He was relieved. But why should he care if Papa had? There was no way Greer could resist someone as perfect for him as Emery, and he'd defend her to anyone. She'd been through something horrific. He didn't know why she'd come to him. He didn't care. She was here and he could easily go all caveman and declare she was his to love and protect. If she wanted that, he would do it. He'd even thump his chest and tell everyone his name was now Maverick.

"No," he said.

"Okay." Papa sounded disappointed. "Nothing on our end either. Thanks for asking."

Greer grunted.

"It's so quiet it worries me. The only good news about that is whoever is after the secret isn't sharing it with the masses. I keep thinking whoever hired Travis, Colby, and Flynn must've hired Emery as well. When is she going to make her move? What if she tries to hurt you? Has she tried to ferret the secret out of you?"

"No." He was again far too forceful. It was a no to all of it. Emery wouldn't hurt him. She wouldn't hurt his family. She was incredible, beautiful, smart, funny, and absolutely perfect to him, and possibly perfect for him. If they could somehow overcome the obstacle of him having shot her brother.

"Okay. I guess we just have to be patient. You're better at that than I am. I hate waiting."

Greer managed a chuckle, but he was all stirred up. How could he explain to Papa how great Emery was? He might have to force out the words.

"Unless you're sick of having this house guest. I know how you like your privacy. I can come pull her out of there, question her, and get to the bottom of it." Papa sounded like he wouldn't mind doing that. He was obviously getting annoyed with the unknown danger.

"No," Greer said again. He swallowed and admitted, "I like her."

There was silence on the line. "What? You like her? Travis Reeder's sister? You *like* her?"

He could almost imagine Papa pacing. He said nothing.

"Greer. You can't go falling in love with Emery Reeder. I should've pulled her out of your house from day one. This is on me. You haven't really dated since Belinda. I wrongly assumed you were still waiting for her."

Greer grimaced. He hadn't told Papa how roughly Belinda had dumped him. He definitely wasn't waiting for her.

"The problem is you're too innocent, good, handsome, intriguing, and I'm sure irresistibly appealing to women. Of course she would be interested in you, or maybe she's preying on you. Ah, I blame myself."

"Stop," Greer said. He forced the next sentences out of his mouth as quick as he could, "She's innocent and good. I don't know why she's here. But I know she would never hurt me or anyone else. No one is taking her from my house. Only she can choose to leave me."

He looked at himself in the bathroom mirror. Emery had pried more words than that out of him the past week, but it was a very long paragraph for him to say to anyone else.

"Wow." Papa whistled. "Greer. You're in love with her, aren't you?"

Greer couldn't admit that, even to himself.

"You don't have to say it. My boy. I wanted to know why she was here and what it meant for the secret, but I never meant to put you in danger like this. Greer, you've got to be smart and careful. You know she's lying to you and hiding a lot from you. She might seem innocent and beautiful, but—"

"Don't," Greer warned. "She is perfect. Don't doubt her." He took a breath, then added, "Or you doubt me."

Silence fell between them. Greer gripped the phone.

Finally Papa said, "Okay. I trusted Colt when he said Bailey wouldn't hurt the family. It didn't play out the way any of us expected, but it did work out. We all know now Bailey was an innocent angel and the perfect one for Colt. I'll trust you too."

"Thank you, Papa," Greer managed. Relief washed over him. Papa would trust him. Of course he would. Now Greer would continue to spend every waking minute with Emery and someday soon they'd share all their secrets. He did love her, but he couldn't say it yet.

"Love you, Greer. I'll be praying for you. I'll be praying for Emery."

"Thanks. Love you."

Greer hung up before Papa got more emotional on him. He loved his Papa, but he didn't need emotion. Unless it was from Emery.

He let himself out of the bathroom and paced his bedroom. His door was open. Emery's door was open. It was almost eleven-thirty. When she had the recurring nightmare, he'd hold her close and kiss her. If she let him, he might hold her close the entire night through.

He prayed as he paced. The good Lord would help him and it would all work out. It had to. He didn't know how he'd go back to his silent, boring existence without Emery.

Somehow, in eight days, she'd become his entire world.

Chapter Thirteen

Emery woke to the sun streaming through the huge bedroom windows. She blinked and rolled over. Savory aromas from the kitchen beckoned to her, and she could hear Greer moving around out there. His tender, delicious, passionate kisses came back to her, and she smiled.

Then it hit her. She hadn't had the nightmare.

She jumped out of bed and raced into the living area. "Greer!" she yelled.

He spun, released the spatula, and hurried to her. "You all right?"

"Yes! I didn't have the nightmare!"

He grinned, picked her up, and spun her around in a circle. Emery threw back her head and laughed. Greer's kisses last night had been magical. Had they cured her of the nightmare? She was so happy. She looked down into his beautiful blue eyes and she wanted to kiss him all over again. His lips could cure her every ill.

Cool air brushed her rear and horror rushed through her. "Please set me down," she begged.

Greer set her down. He was still holding her and smiling. She broke from his hold and backed away. He released her, and his brow furrowed as his smile slid away. "What?"

She tugged at the T-shirt. "You need to turn around or you're going to get a show you didn't pay for."

His eyes widened and he quickly turned around.

Emery all but ran for the bedroom, yelling, "Sorry!" before she slammed the door behind her. She had her clean clothes waiting on the bathroom counter, so she hurried to shower and get dressed. She was almost out of the travel-size toiletries she'd brought with her. Greer had mentioned he needed to go to the grocery store soon. She could ask him to buy her some things, or if she got brave today and told him who she was, she could drop the façade of hiding from her ex and go with him to the store. Greer hadn't referenced her ex at all. She could hardly remember the fake guy's name. It made her think Greer knew who she was. It was time for her to admit it and let him help her figure everything out with the Voice, the Delta family, and her brother's death.

She heard music playing as she walked back through the bedroom. Though he had a nice sound system and speakers built into the house, Greer had only turned music on a few times since she'd been there. Always some country song. She'd never really listened to country before, but she liked how a lot of the songs told a story.

She gingerly opened the door, wanting to observe him for just a moment. He was unloading the clean dishes from the dishwasher and singing along to a song she'd never heard, "God makes five foot nine, brown eyes, and a sundress."

Emery laughed, but he didn't hear her with the music turned up. She missed some of the words, but then Greer sang, "Jack makes good whiskey, but God makes the good stuff. When he made five foot nine, brown eyes, and a ..."

She walked out into the living area and Greer stopped singing.

His eyes widened. He set the cups in his hand down and just stared at her.

"Alexa, stop the music," he said.

Emery smiled at him and tucked her hair behind her ear. She was five foot nine and had brown eyes. This felt like *their* song. "Guess I need a sundress?"

His slow smile came then. "For sure."

She bit at her lip. She wanted to kiss him so badly. He gestured toward the food, but she didn't want food. She wanted him.

They sat down and prayed and ate. Throughout breakfast they talked about Bentley, country music, her not having the nightmare, and what the plan was for the day. Greer admitted he'd stayed up until after midnight waiting for her to scream, but she never had. He seemed thrilled she hadn't had the nightmare, but she knew he woke at five a.m. and worried that he hadn't gotten much sleep. He just smiled like it didn't matter.

The day passed far too quickly. Emery wanted to savor each moment with him. She didn't know what would happen when they both revealed the secrets they'd been hiding. There was no way he could've killed someone as devoted to his country and good to her as Travis had been.

She'd been scared, terrified, petrified, alarmed, frightened to tell him the truth about her coming to him and having the huge can of worms burst open. Now she found she was getting more and more anxious to open up and see what the future held. Her only fear was that everything might implode. What if Greer was mad at her for lying? What if his family had killed Travis and he defended them, tried to convince her Travis was in the wrong?

After dinner, she used the bathroom before they went out for nightly chores and their walk. There was a frustrated text from the voice, *I am so sorry to push you, but we need answers soon. Your time is running out.*

My time? she texted back.

The Deltas are smart. They'll figure out who you are and they'll either kill you or hurt you to get to me. I can't protect you without information. Can't you access his computer or phone?

Emery rolled her eyes. The Voice had tried to be kind, but she didn't believe him any longer. It was most likely his fault Travis was dead. She hadn't met any other Deltas besides Greer, but he was the best of the best and there was a peaceful feeling in this valley. These people couldn't be deluded criminals who would kill her. Who had killed Travis. For all she knew, the Voice had killed her brother and had manipulated both of them for whatever agenda he or his higher ups had.

I'll see what I can find out, she texted back, but truly her only intention tonight was to talk to Greer and sort out the truth from his perspective and the information they each had.

She left her phone in her backpack. Greer was waiting for her in the main area. My oh my, his eyes were really blue and enchanting. They held hands as they went outside. The summer night was glorious, but nothing was as beautiful as Greer.

They worked through the feeding and checked on the cattle together, then held hands as they walked along the lake trail. It was peaceful and perfect. She loved this valley. She'd never had that feeling of home that people talked about, but she could see herself having Christmas and Easter and another Fourth of July here. Raising children here. Growing old here. Most importantly experiencing it all with Greer, her handsome, tough, patient, incredible Maverick.

As they walked, her nerves tingled. It was time. She was ready to spill it all. That she had lied. That the Voice had put her up to it and lied to and used her. That she trusted Greer.

Maybe even that she loved him.

Whew. That was terrifying to think, let alone say. One step at a time.

Greer squeezed her hand. "Can I tell you something?"

"Sure."

She loved that he was talking more and more. He'd never be one to waste words, but he'd gone from one-word answers or at the most a three-word sentence to chatting with her quite well.

Suddenly her heart raced, even though she'd been psyching herself up for this moment. He was going to bring up her lying about being Taylor and then talk to her about Travis's death. Greer had to know who she really was.

"All my animals being named after B," he started with.

She smiled, relieved they could talk about something else first. "Don't forget Boss, the big, beautiful ... uh, green tractor."

He smiled. Then he was quiet for a few beats.

"Why are they all named after B?" she prompted.

The sun was gone behind the mountains. He turned her back toward the house, obviously wanting to get home before it was fully dark. They should skip the movie tonight, talk and then kiss instead.

"A girl ... Belinda."

"Belinda?" She wrinkled her nose, not liking the sound of that name or the fact there was a girl. Which was silly and petty.

"I dated her."

"For how long?"

"Couple years."

Emery didn't like that at all. She was jealous of some woman she'd never met who wasn't a part of Greer's life now. "And you named all your animals after her?"

"She did."

Gross. Emery had thought she was so clever, naming the tractor Boss. "We're changing Boss's name. It's ... Great Green Giant." It was unoriginal, and the tractor wasn't a giant by any means, but she didn't care.

He smiled. "Okay."

"Can I rename all the horses and Brave?" But she liked Brave's name. Dang.

He chuckled. "Sure."

She looked askance at him as they walked. Drawing in a breath, she knew she had to let any jealousy and pettiness go. "Okay, okay," she said, "I'm going to be the bigger, loftier, outstanding, superior, charitable, benevolent, accepting, considerate person here."

He smiled at her list of complimentary to herself synonyms.

"It's not fair to Bear, Bruin, Beau, Brooks, and Brave," she continued, "to confuse them with different names than the names they already know. But we are renaming the tractor."

He pulled her to a stop, turned, and stared deeply into her eyes. His blue eyes got to her every time. Then Greer did something so un-Greer like that she about passed out. He lifted their joined hands to his lips and tenderly kissed her knuckles, letting his lips linger on her flesh.

"I never felt for Belinda like I do for you."

Not only was the sentence long, but the meaning was life-changing. "You're telling me you dated a woman for two years and you never felt for her what you feel for me after nine days?"

"Yes."

They needed to talk about a whole lot of stuff, but now was not the time. Emery flung her arms around his neck and she kissed him. She kissed him very, very passionately.

Greer lifted her off her feet and kissed her back. He kissed her passionately, fervently, ardently, zealously, vehemently—all the good synonyms and all the good feels.

Then he settled her back onto her feet and continued to kiss her.

The kisses took on a life of their own, and neither one of them tried to stop. Darkness fell around them and Emery's face might be more chapped from Greer's beard rubbing against it than her inner thighs had been after wearing shorts on horse rides, even with the blanket.

Finally, she pulled back and could barely see him in the dark.

Greer laughed. "You make me do things I never thought I'd do."

She laughed too.

He pulled out his phone and turned on the flashlight. They made their way back to his barn, where the exterior lights guided them to the house.

As they went inside, Emery only wanted to kiss more. Who cared about some rash on her face from his beard? But suddenly the nerves hit her, and she started shaking. She had to tell him. She had to tell him now. It was past time to clear the air and move forward. Together.

She said a desperate prayer for help.

Greer led her to the couch. "Movie?"

"No. I need to use the bathroom, and then I have to tell you something."

He regarded her, as serious as he'd been when she'd first met him. He knew. Somehow, he knew. But she still had to be the one to say it. That almost made her smile. With Greer, of course she had to be the verbose one, but it was more than that. She needed to prove she trusted him with her secrets, her safety, her life, and her heart.

She hurried away from him and into the bathroom. She brushed her teeth, looked at her reddened cheeks and lips in the mirror, and replayed every minute of those kisses. She used the bathroom, spritzed on some vanilla sugar body splash and put on some lip gloss, and then she dropped to her knees to say a prayer. Somehow, with heaven's help and Greer's kind, patient understanding, she would make it through this.

She was still terrified.

But that was silly. God was on her side, and Greer was an amazing, understanding, and gentle man. He cared more deeply for her than a woman he had dated for two years. She'd never asked why they broke up, but it didn't matter. Unless it had damaged Greer. Maybe that was why he was so quiet.

She walked back out into the main area. Greer was sitting on the couch but he stood, came to her, and escorted her to the couch. Settling down beside her, he waited.

Emery wanted to hold his hand, or better yet sit on his lap, but she needed to say this without any distractions. She stood and started pacing in front of him. Greer stood to face her, but she gently pushed him back onto the couch. "Please. I need to look down on you while I admit to all of this."

He quirked an eyebrow.

"Sorry, that sounded weird. I'm just anxious and with my students I'm taller and I'm always looking down on them and I'm always in control. Well, as in control as you can be with clever nine- and ten-year-olds. But does that make sense?" He didn't look like it did, but he said nothing. "I just need to be ... taller than you for a minute."

"Okay."

"Thanks." She paced and wrung her hands together, then tried to spit it out. "You remember how I ran through the woods and then found you and my ex had gone after me and threatened me and all of that?" She paused her pacing and looked at him. He nodded. "Okay, well, that was ... all a lie."

Greer didn't react. He just kept his blue gaze steadily on her; no anger, no incrimination, no injustice on any part of his face. So Greer.

Suddenly, Emery didn't want to be taller than him. She dropped to her knees in front of him and grabbed both of his hands. She wanted to be humble, meek, respectful, penitent, and most importantly, closer to him.

"Greer ... I'm Emery Reeder."

He squeezed her hands and said, "I know."

Her heart raced. She'd wondered if he knew, but to hear him confirm it was upsetting, liberating, and also awkward. She'd been living this stupid farce, and he'd known the entire time.

"Why didn't you say anything?" She should beg his forgiveness, but the words kind of ripped out of her.

"Emery," he said in a husky voice that made her quiver. He'd said her name. Her real name. He gently tugged her up onto the couch next to him, then angled toward her, still holding both of her hands. "I wanted you to trust me enough to tell me."

There was so much to say, so much to ask, so much to discuss, but those words from Greer brought tears to her eyes. "I do trust you," she said fervently. "With everything, Greer. My Maverick." She gave him a watery, emotional smile. "I trust you with my heart, my body, my soul, my life, my lips."

Greer swallowed and she thought he might kiss her. Sadly, he didn't. "That means a lot."

"You mean a lot," she said softly. She looked him straight in the eyes and said, "I'm so sorry that I listened to the Voice and came here under false pretenses, but I think heaven must've guided my path and everything about us meeting. In nine days ..." She shouldn't do it, but Emery had never been one to hold back. "I've gone from afraid and uncertain to comfortable and attracted to plummeting straight down the tunnel of in love with you, Greer."

He smiled slightly, and then he kissed her. He easily lifted her onto his lap and he kissed her tenderly and beautifully. She savored every moment of it.

When he pulled back, he said, "You don't hate me?"

Emery ran her fingers through his hair and then down to his

broad, strong shoulders. These shoulders would protect her and shelter her from any storm. She'd been right when she'd imagined the analogy of Greer protecting her from the wind, the rain, and the lightning. He was so incredible.

"Hate you? How could I ever hate you? I love you, Greer Delta. I cherish you. I treasure you. I adore you. I revere you. I *savor* you."

He chuckled at that. Then he pulled her close and gave her a long, drugging kiss. She wasn't sure which way was up. She cuddled against his chest after the kiss ended and just relished being close to him, his strength, his unique musk and leather scent, his patience, his goodness.

She needed to tell him all about the Voice tricking her into coming here and find out what they should do next. She needed to ask him if he knew who really killed Travis; if it was the Voice or someone who had lied to the Deltas. If so, they were both in danger. It sounded like his family could help them as well. She was so safe with him and loved him far too much.

The thought of danger was enough to bring her head off his shoulder and the drowsy beauty of peace and love to a stuttering halt. "Greer. We might be in danger. The man who contacted me about you killing Travis." His arms seemed to tighten around her. "He tricked me into coming here. He had a video of Travis talking to me and everything the Voice said about the Navy lined up as well. So I bought into the idea of finishing what Travis had started for our country's protection and avenging my brother's death."

Greer's brow furrowed.

"The Voice—that's what I call him because I have no name— gave me all the information and ideas. He gave me two hundred thousand dollars and a fake ID. I think he's a bad guy, even though he tried to be nice to me. He's been texting me. He wants whatever weapon you and your family are protecting." She drew in a breath and pursed her lips, trying to think how they could find the voice. "Can you trace a text?"

"Papa could."

"Oh, good. Your papa can help keep us safe from him?"

"Yes. My family can."

She breathed out in relief and stared at his handsome face in the dimly lit room. He was so appealing to her. "I know the Voice lied to me about everything. Claiming you killed Travis. How could anybody claim that? You're so good and genuine and pure."

His body stiffened against hers.

"Greer?" she stared at him, and a dart of horror went through her. "Greer?"

He stared at her, but said nothing.

"Greer?" she squeaked.

"Emery," he said softly, his blue eyes filled with pain and regret. He searched her gaze and the seconds dragged on painfully. Emery was terrified of what he was going to say. She wanted to put her hands over her ears and run away screaming.

Greer swallowed and then admitted in a low, gravelly voice, "I did kill Travis."

The thin dart of horror became a raging, massive river of molten lava. Emery shoved herself off his lap. She fell to the floor in a painful heap. Greer reached for her, but she batted his hand away and sprang to her feet, backing up.

Greer stood and faced her. His expression was full of remorse and sorrow, but she could read his face so well and she knew one thing for certain. He was telling the truth.

"You killed my brother?" she gasped out. "Why?"

"He was going to kill my cousin and her boyfriend. I had to."

"You *had* to shoot my only brother in the head, execution style, like some monster? There was no other option to protect your cousin and boyfriend?"

Greer opened his mouth, but she overrode him.

"How could you? How could you murder a loyal, devoted patriot to his country? My brother and protector? How could you?" She was shrieking now. "I talked myself into believing the Voice had lied. I talked myself into believing you were a good guy." She put a hand to her mouth. Her body shook. "How could you kiss me? Pretend you cared about me? You lied to me, betrayed me. You *murdered* my brother."

Greer only shook his head. He didn't say a word.

Emery wanted to yell at him, rant and rave, hit him a whole bunch of times, but she was so sick to her stomach and heartbroken. She had to escape. She'd fallen head over heels for this man and he'd killed her brother. What was wrong with her? What was wrong with him? How could he be so hardened and awful and calloused and devoid of any integrity or emotion to invite her into his house, lie to her that he'd protect her, make her fall in love with him, kiss her like he had? He'd known the entire time that he'd killed her brother. Greer Delta must be a hardened killer and the most impressive liar she'd ever met.

She ran into the bedroom, slammed and locked the door. Sadly, she knew that wouldn't keep him out. She dragged an overstuffed chair in front of the door for good measure. At least that would slow him down. Then she ran to the bathroom and shoved anything of hers into her backpack.

Looking at her phone, she saw she had texts from the Voice, but she didn't know if she could trust him either. She didn't know who she could trust. She had lots of friends, but no one she could turn to in an emergency like this. She had never felt so alone, bereft, scared, and angry in her life.

Kneeling quickly, she prayed for help, strength, protection, and the ability to see clearly. Standing, she stared at herself in the mirror. Her lips and cheeks were red from all the kissing. Her eyes were red, and she hadn't even started the crying fest she wanted to have.

She had to get out of here. That was all she knew. Sadly, she'd have to wait until Greer was asleep to sneak out. She couldn't handle facing him again, and if he tried to touch her or make excuses or claim he cared about her ... she might strangle him.

Chapter Fourteen

Greer knew he should either bang on Emery's door and try to explain why he shot her brother or call Papa and beg him for help. He couldn't bring himself to do either. Instead, he sat on the couch in a stupor for a while, praying for some insight and help. Praying Emery would come back out and talk to him. Praying Emery could someday forgive him.

Forgive him? That would never happen. He pictured the mixture of horror, anger, and revulsion in her beautiful brown eyes directed at him after she'd shoved herself off his lap. It made him want to vomit.

She'd told him she loved him, and then he'd told her the truth. She would never forgive him. What did he expect? He'd done it. He'd shot and killed her only brother.

How had he been stupid enough to think she could forgive him and to let himself fall in love with her? No mortal man could resist an angel like Emery thrust into his life, and especially not an inexperienced man like him. Like Papa said, he hadn't really dated since

Belinda. What did he know about love and relationships besides what he read in books or watched his family members experience?

He stood and walked to Emery's door. He didn't know what he should or could say, but he had to try. It might be smarter to let her rest and see if he had a clearer head in the morning, but he couldn't stand to leave things as they were.

He heard movement inside the room. That encouraged him. At least she hadn't crawled out the window or locked herself in the bathroom.

"Emery?" he called through the door.

No answer. No movement. Complete stonewall.

He knocked on the door again. "Emery?"

No way was he going to pick open the lock. Not now.

He thought he heard a sniffle from inside the room. She was crying? Who could blame her? She'd so sweetly told him, "I love you, Greer Delta. I cherish you. I treasure you. I adore you. I revere you. I *savor* you."

Ah, Emery. He wanted to proclaim every one of those terms back to her, but now was not the time for that. Maybe someday.

He shook his head. Probably not in this lifetime.

"I'm sorry about your brother's death," he said to the door. "You have no idea how sorry." He drew in a breath and he had no clue if she was listening, but he started spewing words like he'd never done in his life. "Your brother and two of his friends were hired to go after … something my family is protecting. They attacked my brother Thor and his girlfriend Shelly to find out the location of the secret, but Thor overpowered them and they got arrested."

He paused and thought he could hear her breath. At least she wasn't yelling at him or running away.

"One of the guy's mom posted bail. Shortly after, the three of them kidnapped my cousin Alivia and her boyfriend to force her to take them to the secret. They escaped after a day and a half, ran, and found shelter in an old cabin. My cousin Colt, my uncle Joseph, and I were one of the groups searching for them."

He took a breath and could've sworn he could hear her panting gasps on the other side of the door. He prayed she was listening, but he didn't know if his explanation would help anything.

"We heard gunshots. Lots of gunshots. We raced that direction and found Travis and his friends shooting up the front of the cabin with some serious firepower."

A gasp. She was there, and she was listening.

"We started shooting at them as we approached and everything went insane. Uncle Joseph shot Flynn Wright and killed him. Colt and I tackled Colby Newman and Travis disappeared."

Would she call him a liar? Tell him she hated him? Only silence sounded from the bedroom. Had she walked away so she wouldn't hear this? He continued anyway.

"Colt told me to go, so I ran for the cabin. As I reached the window, I heard your brother say, 'It's time to die,' and then he pointed his gun at Alivia and Klein. I reacted instinctively to protect them. I shot him."

"No!" Emery screamed. "No, no, no!"

Greer heard something being dragged across the floor, and then the door flung open. Emery stood there, breathing hard. Her dark curls were wild around her face and her eyes were red-rimmed. The skin around her mouth was slightly red and her lips were swollen. She was so beautiful it hurt to look at her.

"No!" she yelled, pointing a finger at him but backing up as if afraid he'd reach for her. "You're a liar and a murderer. My brother would never take a bribe like a mercenary, kidnap people, and then try to kill them in cold blood. He was a soldier. He loved and served our country and he was on a special ops mission. Your family is deluded; you think you're protecting some stupid secret for your country but you're on the wrong side, Greer Delta!"

Greer blinked at her. Did she really believe that? Or was she just spewing angry words? "I'm sorry, Emery. Whoever the Voice is ... he's after the secret. He used and manipulated your brother, and now he's trying to use and manipulate you."

She stared him down, or rather up. "So my brother's a stupid dupe who went AWOL from the Navy and let some jerk control him and then became a kidnapping, murderous villain for money?"

Greer shrugged. All he knew of Travis Reeder was he had gone AWOL, had taken a million dollars with the promise of five million more to find the secret, and he'd resorted to kidnapping and attempted murder not just with Alivia and Klein but also with Greer's brother Thor and his now-fiancée Shelly. What could he say? The only good thing he knew about Travis Reeder was currently glaring at him.

"My brother was a good man, and you killed him," she said in a low, trembling voice. "I hate you, Greer Delta." Those beautiful brown eyes of hers were cold and angry. The way she looked at him hurt as much as her words. "I loathe you, I abhor you, I despise you, I detest you, I'm revolted by you ... Ugh!" She threw her hands in the air. "I can't think of any more words. Just stay away from me."

She slammed the door again.

Greer's heart felt like it had been ripped in two. He'd tried to explain, and she'd refused to listen. What else could he do? Would she calm down in the morning? Did it even matter? Even if she came to believe what her brother was capable of, how could she possibly love Greer knowing he'd killed her flesh and blood?

Over the past nine days he'd let himself push the insurmountable obstacle between them away as they'd grown close. He'd fallen in love with the irresistible Emery Reeder. It had been idiotic of him. Papa was right. Papa should've taken Emery away from Greer as soon as she'd appeared, questioned her, and sent her back to Mesquite. It would've avoided so much heartache for both of them.

Rubbing at the tightness in his forehead, Greer slowly made his way across the great room, through his bedroom, and into his bathroom. He started the shower, hoping the hot water would soothe his aching head, shoulders, and heart.

Who was he kidding? Nothing could soothe his heart. Emery despised him, and nobody could blame her. Least of all him.

Chapter Fifteen

Emery was so angry she was shaking all over. Her heart thumped out of control and her head pounded as she paced her room. What should she do? How could she escape?

She should pray, but she was too distraught. How could her only Father, her Heavenly Father whom she trusted and loved, put her in a situation like this? She had felt inspired to come here. She couldn't deny it. Maybe the Voice was partly to blame and she was an idiot for listening and being guilted into avenging her brother and helping her country. She was an idealistic, trusting fool. Mostly regarding one Greer Delta.

Greer had shot and killed her brother. Shot him right through the head. How dare he try to portray Travis as some bad guy?

You saw the darkness in him after his last deployment, a quiet voice murmured.

"No!" she yelled aloud. She would not let the devil make her think her brother was a bad guy. It was one thing that Travis had struggled with whatever happened on his last deployment, but that meant he was good and it had hurt him to have to follow orders and probably take life.

No way could Travis, who'd been her rock and her shelter through childhood and even teenage years, be a mercenary who would desert his military duties and resort to kidnapping and almost killing someone for money. She couldn't believe that of the brother who'd watched out for her throughout her childhood.

Greer. He was to blame. He'd taken her brother from her.

"Agh!" she screamed. She had to get out of here. She'd go home, back to her students, back to her hot, miserable existence in Mesquite. Without Greer. Definitely without Greer. Goodness, why would she want Greer? The murdering liar anyway.

"I hate him, I loathe him, I abhor him, I despise him, I detest him. I'm revolted by him, appalled by him, repulsed by him, nauseated by him, intrigued by him, impressed by him, obsessed with him ..." She ripped off a thumbnail with her teeth and screamed out, "Why? Why do I always go there?"

Muttering the most despicable synonyms of evil she could think of to override the few good descriptors that had sneakily crept into her list, she kept pacing. When she ran out of words, she closed her eyes and leaned against the wall.

Please help me, Lord.

The prayer was insincere, but it was all she could manage.

She could hear water running through the wall. That brought her head up. Water running? Could Thor be showering? She could escape before he fell asleep. She looked at her phone. There were even more messages from the Voice and some from college friends and teacher friends she hadn't responded to this week.

She ignored them all.

It was nine-fifty. If she stole one of Greer's vehicles, she might make it to Grand Junction, ditch his vehicle, and retrieve her car before he put out a police track thingy to find her.

She didn't think he'd come check on her again tonight after their last confrontation. Hopefully he wouldn't hear the garage open while he showered. She had to try. Maybe that running water was the answer to her prayer.

Grabbing her backpack, she crept out of her room, darting her gaze to Thor's open bedroom door. The shower was indeed running. She hurried across the great room, through the mudroom, and out into his large garage. It was dark, but she wasn't about to flip a light on. What should she take? The Tesla would be fast, but she'd heard owners could track those and police probably watched for people speeding in them. She didn't want to be on a dirt bike or in a side by side that was open. The four-door truck it was.

She climbed in, trying not to think about how it smelled like Greer and his leather and musk deliciousness.

Not delicious. Disgusting. Revolting. Nauseating. Repelling.

She pushed the garage door opener and was impressed with how quietly it went up. Whoever built Thor's house had done quality work. Wait. It was his cousin, the woman builder he'd told her about.

Alivia. The very woman Greer had supposedly saved from her supposedly-murderous, villainous brother.

How could her brother have tried to kill a woman? No. He wouldn't.

A scene from her nightmare suddenly flashed in her mind. Travis stabbing the beautiful blonde woman. The beautiful blonde woman with Greer's blue eyes. No!

Despair made it hard to see clearly. She backed out of the garage, shut the door, and put it into drive. At first she drove slowly and prayed Greer's family wouldn't see her, that Greer wouldn't come chasing after her, but all was quiet. She skirted around the lake, past a grouping of his family's houses, and then down the canyon, checking her rearview mirror for lights every other second.

When she finally hit the canyon at the south end of Summit

Valley, she breathed a little easier. Gripping the steering wheel, she drove five miles over the speed limit. The speed limit felt far too slow, but she'd never gotten pulled over for five miles over. A speeding ticket at this point could be fatal.

She tried to relax and focus on the dark road. Even with how angry she was at Greer and his family and the injustice of Travis's death, she didn't believe Greer would ever hurt her. She could picture his blue eyes staring deeply at her, feel his arms around her, his lips on hers.

"Gah! Stop, brain!"

Finally, she got out of that canyon and to Highway 50. A passing sign informed her she was a hundred miles from Grand Junction. Probably closer to an hour and a half at this speed. Would Greer discover she was gone? A stupid part of her wanted him to chase after her, convince her he was genuine, tell her he loved her. She'd stupidly told him she loved him, in far too many ways, but he'd never said it back. She could swear it had been in his eyes, though.

It didn't matter. She couldn't love her brother's killer. She had to root these traitorous feelings out. Get back to normal life. Somehow pay the Voice back for the money she'd spent, return the rest of it, and be free of the guy who had given Travis and his friends the assignment to steal some secret.

Travis had been honorable about what he'd done. He had to have been.

If Greer was right, he'd been a mercenary who'd sold his soul and been willing to kill an innocent woman and her boyfriend. Greer had said it all so nonjudgmentally, matter-of-factly, exactly the way her Greer would.

Dang it, Greer. Why couldn't he just be some normal guy she'd met out on her morning walk or at the sandwich shop? Maybe a fellow teacher or a firefighter who had come to school to do a presentation?

They could've been so happy together. Emery didn't know if she'd ever recover from falling in love so quickly and deeply and thinking Greer was the best man in the world to then having it all ripped out from under her.

She had to stop thinking about it. Now.

She pushed the button to turn the radio on. Of course it was on a country song. She liked the guy's voice, and it was catchy. She'd learned to love country music over the past nine days with Greer.

"God made her, so I will make sure he didn't waste an angel on me."

The singer paused, and she was intrigued about the sweetness of this cowboy calling his girl an angel. Would Greer call her an angel?

"When he made five-feet nine, brown eyes, and a sundress."

"No!" she screamed, pushing the button off, but the lyrics still bounced in her head and worst of all, she could see Greer singing them, and he looked as appealing as ever.

Ah, crap. She didn't dare turn the station back on and risk hearing more. She'd have to deal with silence until she got to her own car. Every station of Greer's SiriusXM radio was bound to be set to some country song that would remind her of him.

Dang Greer Delta. Dang him all to purgatory.

She loathed him.

And she wished she could hear him sing again, and that she could wear a sundress for him.

Chapter Sixteen

Greer took a long, long shower. It didn't help clear his brain, but it felt good on his aching forehead, neck, and shoulders. Nothing could help his aching heart, though. Nothing but Emery, and she wouldn't soften to him. Ever.

He wrapped a towel around his waist and looked at himself in the mirror. He looked tired. He was tired. His eyes were red-rimmed and his lips were slightly swollen. Ah, Emery. Those kisses. But she was so much more than his physical attraction or even the incredible connection and powerful emotions when they touched or kissed. She was everything to him. More than he'd ever dreamed or hoped for.

He loved her. Had he even told her that? He hung his head. Nope. It wouldn't surprise anyone who knew him that he hadn't forced words out when he should have.

Why hadn't he told in every synonym he could think of that he loved, adored, cherished, and revered her?

Yet when he'd tried to explain through the bedroom door, talking much more than he ever did, it had caused all the anger obviously building inside of her to explode. Would him telling her he loved her have done the same?

He took a long breath, closed his eyes, and prayed. He'd have to give it until morning, pray she could forgive him, pray they could work things out, that she would somehow believe him about what Travis had attempted to do, that he could tell her how he felt about her. But he didn't hold out much hope. She hated him, with lots of different synonyms.

His phone buzzed on the bathroom counter. It was quarter past ten, so it automatically wouldn't ring. He turned it over and saw it was Papa. Blowing out a breath, he didn't want to answer. Could he just send Papa a text that he needed to sleep? The only person he wanted to talk to right now was Emery. Did he need to tell Papa everything that had gone wrong and that the Voice, whoever that guy was, might come after them? What if Emery had texted the man and told him to come after the Deltas?

The phone stopped buzzing. He held it up to his face and swiped it open. His eyes widened. The phone icon showed seven missed calls and ten texts waiting to be read. What was going on? He clicked on the phone and saw two missed calls from Papa and five from his dad. He clicked on Papa's number.

"Greer. You okay?"

"Yeah. Are you?"

"Yes. I'm almost to your house to check if it's secure. Where are you going and why didn't you answer your phone?"

"Going? I just got out of the shower."

"The cameras show your truck leaving your garage a little before ten. We didn't get a notice of anyone walking through the main area as it was before ten, but your dad saw you drive past and tried to call you repeatedly. When you didn't answer, he called me to look through the cameras. I looked at the garage cam. It was dark, but I saw your truck pull out."

Greer rushed to his closet and started sliding into a T-shirt. "Living room camera?"

"Let me pull it up. I didn't want to watch any ... private moments."

He appreciated that, but if Emery had taken his truck and was running from him ...

Please keep her safe, he begged heaven above.

"Okay. It shows you going to your room and ... about fifteen minutes later, nine-fifty-one, Emery walking through the living area for the mudroom and garage. She's got her backpack."

Greer wanted to curse. He finished dressing, grabbed his wallet and shoved it in his pocket, and ran for his garage.

"What are you going to do?" Papa asked.

"Go after her."

"Do you want me, your dad, or Thor to come with you?"

"No."

"How do you know where she's going?"

That slowed Greer's steps as he reached his Tesla, quickly unplugged the battery cable, and then rushed around and jerked open the door. She'd taken his truck. At least she'd left him the faster car. "I don't."

"I'll put out a request with highway patrol. If they find your truck or her car that she left in Grand Junction, they'll let me know and stay with her if they can, but they won't stop her. Unless you want them to?"

"I need to be the one." He slid into the car and pushed the garage remote and then the start button.

"Okay. Good luck, Greer. She's running from you. Does that mean she's trusting whoever sent her?" Papa paused but didn't seem to expect an answer. Greer didn't know. He sped out of the garage, flipped around, and took off into the night. "She might be in danger for not fulfilling her assignment," Papa mused. "Did she tell you anything about her instructions before...?"

Before it all went sideways, or backwards, or worse.

"She doesn't know his name. Calls him the Voice. He's after the secret." Greer flew through the valley and to the canyon. "Paid her two hundred grand."

"That's all you know?"

"Yep."

"Okay. Find her. Keep her safe. We'll figure it out. If she has his number, maybe we can track it."

Greer nodded and pushed the end call button. He didn't want to talk. He wanted to drive and focus on finding Emery.

Twenty minutes later, he was out of Summit Valley and racing down the 50. Blue and red lights appeared in his rearview. Greer wasn't a curser. He cursed.

He pulled over quickly, figuring the faster he dealt with the highway patrol, the better. He or Papa should've thought to put out a notice about Greer's car, too.

The guy sauntered up. "Know how fast you were going, son?"

Greer shook his head.

"One-thirty-seven." The man eyed him. He looked surprisingly congenial for catching Greer going more than double the speed limit. "I try to keep things chill, but that is a ridiculous speed. I hate to take your license, but I definitely could."

Greer grimaced. He couldn't afford this delay.

"You weren't swerving, and you don't look high or drunk."

Greer appreciated the patrolman giving him the benefit of the doubt.

"So what's the excuse for treating my highway like a racetrack?"

"Emergency."

The guy's eyebrows shot up. "What's the nature of your emergency, son?"

Greer shook his head. He couldn't share anything with some stranger, no matter if he was an officer of the law and had been more than reasonable considering how fast Greer was going.

"You won't tell me?" The man looked surprised.

He shook his head again.

The guy studied him. Greer met his gaze and prayed harder than he ever had. He should beg this guy, but he'd never begged anyone in his life. He was going to beg Emery for forgiveness, but that was a whole different story. A cowboy could grovel to the love of his life and still hold his head up like a man.

"Please," he said. "Write me a ticket."

"A ticket?" The guy chortled at that. "You're cruising *my* highway at a buck thirty-seven and you think you'll get off with a ticket? You're in a sixty-five mile per hour zone, by the way, but I'm sure your fancy car tells you that. You're more than double the speed limit and you want me to just write you a ticket so you can get to your unnamed 'emergency'?"

Greer nodded.

The guy looked him over like he was an abnormality. "I have been more than patient with you, son. You should be *begging* me for mercy. Anybody else in the world would do a whole heap of begging right about now."

"Please," Greer grunted out.

"You are something else. If you weren't going seventy-two miles over the speed limit, I might be impressed by your lack of groveling. But as it is, you are going to tell me what this emergency is, and it had better be a doozy, or I'll suspend your license, arrest you, and impound your car."

Greer closed his eyes. This was escalating, and all he could think about was he had to get to Emery. He reached down to pull out his phone.

"Whoa, keep your hands where I can see them!"

"Phone," Greer said, glad his pistol and holster were still underneath the console. "Call Papa."

The phone connected in the car. "Calling Papa Delta," it said.

"Get out of this car," the officer demanded, any former patience and curiosity gone. "You're gonna call daddy and think he can get you out of the mess you've created?"

Greer pushed open the door as the officer stepped back. He stood as Papa answered through the Bluetooth. "Greer, why are you stopped?"

"Highway patrol," he told Papa. He pushed the button to take it off the car's speaker and put it to his ear.

"What? Ah, sorry, I wasn't thinking with everything going on. I'll have to call in a clearance. Let me talk to him."

"Give me that phone," the man demanded at the same time. He looked up at Greer as Greer handed over the phone. "A big cowboy, huh? Wouldn't figure you for driving a Tesla."

Greer would've laughed, remembering Emery teasing him about a sissy car and wearing pink underpants, but his heart hurt too badly.

The man put the phone to his ear and said amicably enough, "Well, Papa Bear, is it?"

Papa must've launched in immediately because the guy shut up and listened. He strode away from Greer, back to his sport utility. The conversation sounded animated. Then the guy slammed himself into his driver's seat. At least that meant he knew Greer wasn't a danger to him. Greer wanted to take off, but he couldn't leave his phone or risk getting arrested. Even Papa had limits to what he could do.

Greer paced around his car. A few cars drove past, but it was quiet at this time of night. The summer night air was a perfect temperature, but nothing was perfect for him.

Almost twenty minutes passed. Precious minutes. Who knew where Emery was or if she was okay? What if she crashed driving because she was angry with him? What if she was heading to the Voice and the guy hurt her?

Finally, finally, the officer's door opened and he slowly approached. He placed the phone into Greer's palm and gave him a serious but curious look. "Your Papa is quite the impressive guy."

Greer nodded.

The man pursed his lips, and a muscle worked in his jaw. "I've been instructed to let you get to your *emergency*. You slow it down though, you got me?"

Greer couldn't lie to him. "No, sir."

The guy looked him over and then grinned. "She must be some woman."

Greer could only nod. Emery was. She was incredible, and he'd ruined everything.

The guy shook his head. "Strong, silent type. Well, go get her, and maybe open your mouth and try a little groveling when you find her, but don't kill somebody driving."

"Yes, sir."

The man lifted a hand and strode back to his vehicle. Greer felt bad for the guy. He was just trying to keep his highway safe. Greer would drive safely... at well over a hundred miles per hour. Emery's safety was more important than his own.

Three more times on the Colorado highways, lights came on behind him. He'd groan every time, but thankfully the lights would turn off and the highway patrol would fade away before Greer could pull over.

Papa called and said the police had found his abandoned truck at the storage unit Emery had parked her car at nine days ago. Or was it ten now? Then he had confirmation that Utah police had seen her Camry and matched the plates. She had to be heading to her home in Mesquite.

Greer hit the Utah border at about two a.m. His eyes were gritty and he needed to pee, but he would not stop. Two different police came after him in Utah, but they also faded away. Then he heard the annoying beep. His Tesla could go over four-hundred miles without needing to be charged, and he had almost reached that limit.

Shoot. He found a station not far away. It took twenty minutes of precious time, but he used the bathroom, splashed cold water on his face, and bought himself a Snickers, a water bottle, and a Rockstar to give him some energy. He downed the candy bar and the drinks so fast he almost choked and then he thought of Emery teasing him about slowing down and savoring his food. He longed to be near her again.

He strode back to the Tesla and unplugged it. Before he settled into the seat, he opened the console, strapped on his hip holster, loaded his Smith & Wesson .500, and slipped it in. He wanted to be prepared when he got to Emery's. He was probably being overly cautious, and he was probably just exhausted and now had too much caffeine racing through his veins, but he was concerned.

Finally he got back on the road, anxious to find Emery and terrified the Voice would find her first.

He was cruising through the southern Utah town of St. George, almost to the Nevada border when the lights came on behind him. It made his stomach turn every time, but they always went away. He kept racing along the freeway, but this police car stayed right with him.

Greer pushed out a heavy breath and knew he needed to pull over.

He rested his head on the steering wheel as the guy came up to his window and banged on it. Greer pushed the automatic window button and looked at him through bleary eyes.

"I don't care who you are or what kind of clearance you think you have. One-forty-two through my town will not be tolerated."

Oh, boy. Greer had a bad feeling. This guy was ready to throttle him. Could Papa's connections even get him out of this one?

"Get out of the car," the guy demanded.

Greer pushed out of the door and stood.

"You're carrying, are you, big guy?" The guy looked pointedly at the pistol on Greer's hip. "You just try to pull that on me and I'll kill you without blinking."

Greer said nothing, though he knew he probably had better training. His reaction time and accuracy always impressed everybody who saw him draw and shoot. As evidenced by how quickly he'd shot Travis.

"Put the gun in the car."

Pulling the gun slowly out, Greer set it back in the car and then turned to the officer.

The guy glared up at him. "Now start talking and start talking fast. Why are you burning through my town and why do I have a notice that I'm supposed to let you cruise on through like it's your personal parade route?"

Greer shook his head. "Emergency."

"I'll give you an emergency. You can explain to me what's going on or I can arrest you and let your high-up official come and get you out. How do you like that?"

Greer tried for humble. "Sir. I'm sorry."

"Not yet, you're not."

Greer took a deep breath. He'd never had a problem with a police officer in his life. Sheriff Reed Peterson was a friend to him and his family. He could completely understand this guy being mad that he'd been going so fast through his town and not liking somebody higher up telling him he had to permit it, but Greer was only twenty minutes from Mesquite and Emery. Even though she didn't want him around, he was certain she needed him. He had to get to her.

"Please," he said in the most conciliatory tone he'd ever used.

The guy blinked at him. "Why don't you try to walk in a line and we'll see how long I can detain you?"

Greer held in a groan and hoped he didn't sway as he walked. With how tired and anxious he was, he was about ready to fall over.

Chapter Seventeen

Emery was exhausted when she finally got to her cottage early the next morning. She'd left Greer's truck and switched to her car at Grand Junction before midnight and it was less than a six-hour drive at that point. Even with a stop to pee and get gas.

She tried to lie down on her bed, but sleep wouldn't come. Finally, she got up and soaked in the tub, then put on a comfortable white sundress and wandered around her small home. Why she put on a sundress, she wouldn't let herself analyze.

She should go on a walk or try to sleep or call ... who would she call? She didn't know if she could share the story with any of her friends. All she wanted was to talk to Greer. But that was dumb.

Rolling her eyes at herself, she made some eggs and toast and forced herself to eat. Her phone rang. She snatched it up. The Voice. This nightmare was over, and it was time to be done with this guy. She had to stand up to him at some point.

"Where are you?" he demanded.

Interesting. Apparently the compassionate Voice was gone.

"Home. I'm out."

"You're *out*? I'll tell you when you're out." He was yelling now. It was scary, but also a relief that he wasn't trying to snowball her with his fake kindness and platitudes.

"I'm sorry," he immediately backtracked. "Forgive me. I'm just so anxious that the Deltas not hurt or kill anyone else like they did Travis ... and my son."

Emery froze. He'd mentioned his son earlier. The poor man had lost a child. "I'm ... sorry," she managed. She sank into the sofa in her living room, her legs too shaky to support her.

"Me too." His voice was soft, full of sorrow. "I wasn't part of my son's life, but I watched Flynn from afar. He excelled in the Navy, and I was very proud. I thought this mission might be his chance to prove the caliber of soldier he was and receive advancements he wouldn't otherwise be considered for. I knew with Travis along he couldn't fail. It was my fault. I shouldn't have sent them." His voice caught. "I would've gone myself, but she wouldn't let me ..."

Who was *she*? The man's boss? His son had been Travis's friend and killed as well. And the Voice blamed himself. The poor guy.

"I'm sorry about your son," she managed.

"I'm sorry about your brother."

Silence came on the phone. She felt awkward and awful. But she wasn't going after whatever the secret was, no matter how guilty she felt about Travis and this man's son.

"I'm sorry I can't get the secret for you," she said quietly.

"Emery, you have to. You're our only hope." His voice was begging. "Please. Do it for your country. Do it for Travis. Do it for Flynn."

"I can't. I left."

"Word is that Greer Delta has been racing across Colorado and Utah to find you."

"Greer's coming here?" Her heart leaped. She tried not to get excited about seeing Greer. Could it mean he loved her despite everything? She had to forget about love right now, or maybe forever where Greer was concerned.

"He is. This is your chance, Emery. He's chasing you and he obviously cares deeply for you. Find out where the weapon is hidden and you could save so many lives."

Emery was more confused than ever. She didn't know that she could ever forgive Greer for killing Travis, but she'd been praying for the spirit of discernment and now she could clearly hear the falseness in the Voice's voice. She believed his son had been killed and he felt deep sorrow for the loss, but he was lying about other things and he was desperate to get the weapon.

"I won't do it," she said. "Whatever this weapon is, whatever Travis believed he was fighting for, I don't trust you or know you."

Quick breaths were her only answer.

"No matter what Greer has done"—she couldn't believe she was saying this—"I trust him. I know him. He's good all the way through. I don't understand why he shot my brother, but I do know the weapon in your hands would be far more dangerous than in the Deltas' hands." Maybe it was a shot in the dark but as she said the words she felt the truthfulness of them. This man wanted the weapon for his own agenda and purposes, not to save America.

There was silence, and then the Voice came as a snarl. "You get the information I need from Greer Delta, or you will both die."

Then he hung up.

Emery stared at the phone. The Voice had just threatened to kill her and Greer. She'd instinctively known he was lying, and he'd just confirmed he was evil. Had he used her brother? She thought he'd lied to and used Travis and his own son, ultimately causing their deaths. For his own purposes or whoever his boss was, a she?

It was too much to muddle out, but she had to tell Greer everything the Voice had said and let him make sense of it. Was he truly coming? The words to that song played through her head as she looked down at her sundress. She couldn't be thinking about country songs and her tenderness for Greer right now.

She looked out her front window. The flowers in her window boxes were still blooming. Had her sweet neighbor Amanda watered them this entire time?

A black Tesla pulled up to the sidewalk in front of her house. Emery's eyes widened and her heart beat high and fast. She didn't move as Greer climbed out of the car, back-lit by the rising sun. Her breath rushed out.

He looked so incredibly good. Tall and strong and wearing his pistol on his hip like he always did around his ranch. The first moment she'd met him, that pistol had terrified her, but then she'd learned how good he was.

What about him killing Travis and all the anger, hatred, and resentment that had fueled her screaming at him and running from him last night?

She didn't know how to reconcile all the conflicting emotions and confusing stories. Even though the Voice had revealed he was lying and she'd always thought he had his own agenda, she still was spitting mad at Greer. He'd killed her brother.

As Greer strode up the walk, she saw that he actually didn't look good. He looked tired and disheveled and concerned. Ah, Greer. No matter what, he looked amazing to her.

Could she resolve loving the man who'd killed her brother? Not anytime soon, she couldn't.

The doorbell rang. She couldn't think about her messed-up relationship and feelings right now. She had to stop the Voice from killing them both and stealing some weapon from the Deltas.

Her jaw tightened. He'd even said he blamed himself for his son, Flynn, and Travis being in the situation. Was he or his boss to blame? His threat after pretending to be so kind made him sound unhinged

154

and extremely dangerous. Maybe losing his son had put him over the edge.

Shakily, Emery walked to the door and swung it wide. Greer's blue eyes met hers and all the worries and anger and sadness disappeared. His eyes were bloodshot and he looked so tired and beat up. She wanted to hold him close, but her feelings about her brother and the entire mess were too raw. Had he really raced through the night to get to her?

"Emery," he murmured in a husky tone that sent shivers through her.

She stepped back and gestured him inside, surprising herself by not yelling at him again. "You're not safe," she whispered. "Get in here."

His eyebrows rose, but he obeyed. She shut and locked the door, then turned to him. She wanted to say so many things, but she tried to focus on the essentials. "The Voice said he'll kill both of us if I don't find out the secret location of your weapon and tell it to him."

Greer studied her. She felt her face flare. That had sounded like a dramatic line from a spy novel. Sparks crackled between them and it was hard not to get distracted with the need to throw herself against his beautiful chest, to feel the protection, safety, comfort, and excitement only Greer could offer her.

"I'll keep you safe," he said. He touched his hip, and she glanced at the gun he had strapped on. Was it the gun that had killed Travis? She'd gotten used to him wearing a pistol when they worked on his ranch and rode the perimeter of his property, and she knew Greer would never hurt her. He'd only protect her.

She blinked at him, wanting to cry, wanting to hold him, but knowing she couldn't. "I know you will." She backed up a step so she wouldn't do something irrational like hug him. He'd treated her so kindly when she was at his home. She tried to return the favor despite the angst pulsing through her. "You're probably exhausted. What do you need? A drink? A nap? Some food? The bathroom's dusty from me being gone, but it's semi-clean."

He smiled slightly at her and her stomach flip-flopped. "The Voice's phone number."

"Oh. Yeah." She opened the contact and handed the phone over to Greer. Their fingers brushed, and she jolted. He affected her every which way.

He gave her a longing look that yanked at her heart before pulling out his phone and texting the number to somebody. He handed her phone back, and she carefully took it without touching him.

"Well, let's get you some food and something to drink and then you can nap while we wait for your papa to figure this out."

Or for the Voice to show up and try to kill them both.

That was silly. The Voice shouldn't be anywhere near here.

She tried to smile at Greer, but every part of her was shaky. She was so angry at him and part of her hated him for killing her brother and trying to objectively explain it to her last night.

"You've been taking care of me for nine days. I guess it's time to return the favor," she said when he only studied her with those penetrating blue eyes of his. "I have to warn you, though. The food in the fridge is probably all expired. Except the eggs. Eggs last a long time, right? And I just pulled a loaf of bread out of the freezer."

She couldn't handle him looking at her any longer. It was a begging look. A *please forgive me* look. A *please love me* look.

Pushing out a breath, she turned toward the kitchen. Greer's hand on her arm stopped her, and she paused and stared up at him. Her traitorous body filled with warmth from the simple touch.

"I'm sorry," he said.

She blinked at him. A few moments passed, then she admitted, "I know you are."

Did him being sorry change anything? Could she forgive him?

"Can you ever forgive me?" he asked, as if he'd read her mind.

Emery didn't know. She shrugged and said, "It's a lot, Greer. It's heavy, jarring, intense, loaded ... it's too much to simply forgive you and go back to the way we ..."

He swallowed and his gaze darted to her lips before meeting her eyes again. She wanted to kiss him so badly. She wanted him to hold her while she cried for Travis's loss one more time, or maybe a dozen more times. She wanted a lot of things from him that she couldn't focus on right now.

"I need time, Greer."

It was a flimsy excuse. She needed a lot more than time.

"How long?"

"Weeks, months, years ... I don't know. I honestly might never come to grips with you killing my brother." It was harsh, but it was true.

He nodded and lifted his hand from her arm. His blue eyes were full of sadness.

Emery pulled in a breath and had to turn away from him. She busied herself getting them both some eggs and toast while he used the bathroom and downed two cups of water.

She'd already eaten, but she forced herself to eat a few bites while he ate quickly. The silence between them was stifling. Emery hated it. She hated how awkward things felt. She wished she could tell him she would come to grips with everything, but it was overwhelming.

His phone rang halfway through breakfast.

"Excuse me," he murmured.

He stood and walked back into the living room. Emery tried to listen in, but with Greer's one-word answers, she didn't get any kind of information. Greer had gradually grown more verbose with her during the time she'd stayed with him, but obviously whoever he was talking to didn't get much out of him.

Her back door slammed open.

A man carrying a pistol darted in. Emery barely registered his black ski mask. She cried out and stumbled to her feet and away from him, but she wasn't fast enough. The guy yanked her against his side and shoved the pistol against her forehead with his other hand. Terror made her muscles lock, and she froze in his arms.

Greer appeared in the kitchen doorway, his gun in his hand. "Don't," he warned the guy.

"Don't you tell me what to do," the man yelled, and Emery recognized his voice. He was *the* Voice. Her stomach dropped to her toes. "You're going to tell me where the weapon is, or I'll kill her and then I'll go after your mama or somebody you actually care about."

Greer's gaze focused on her. His blue eyes were so full of her, and she knew she was his world. She was in mortal danger, but all she could see was Greer. He was her tough, protective cowboy and he would never let anything happen to her. She was safe with him.

"I love you, Emery," Greer said.

Emery's heart raced out of control. He'd said the words, and right before she would probably die.

"What?" the Voice yelled. "Who cares? I'm going to kill her. I'm not messing around here. Go ahead and say your goodbyes. You obviously don't care about her enough to reveal the weapon for her. What a pathetic excuse for a boyfriend."

Greer watched the man steadily as he ranted, not responding or so much as flinching.

"Fine," the Voice sneered. "Your uncle killed my son. Now I'll kill her for recompense. Then no one is going to stop me. I'm coming to your valley, and I'll kill Deltas until I find somebody you actually care about."

The Voice was going insane, and he was going to kill her. She knew it. Emery wanted to tell Greer she loved him, but her throat was so dry and tight and the fear so overwhelming that she couldn't even speak.

Greer dipped his chin slightly. Emery felt the terror fill her, but during their time together, she had learned to hear what he wasn't saying. She dropped to the ground a split second before a gunshot pierced the air.

She screamed.

The Voice's body slammed against her counter and then hit the floor. Blood seeped out of his forehead, saturating his mask. His eyes behind the mask were wide and unseeing.

Emery tried to scramble away. Greer was right there. He holstered his gun, helped her up, and then escorted her out of the kitchen and into the living room. He held her against his chest with his left arm, pulled his phone out with his right, and pushed a button on it.

A second later, he said, "Papa. I killed Flynn Wright's father. I think he was the Voice." He looked to Emery for confirmation, and she dipped her chin shakily.

Papa said a bunch of words, but none of them registered in Emery's mind. All she could see was that blood and the unseeing eyes. Was that how Travis had looked?

Greer pocketed the phone sometime later. Then he turned her into him and held her tight while her body shook with sobs. "You're okay," he said softly.

Emery looked up at him. "No, I am not," she whispered, and then her volume increased. "I am *not* okay. You killed him." She brought her fists up and pounded on his chest. "You killed that man. You killed Travis. Why are you a killer? How can you just coldly shoot somebody? I love you, and I don't want you to be a killer."

Greer blinked at her while she had her tirade. He didn't seem upset or violent or dangerous. "I had to protect you," he said simply.

Emery cried harder. She wrapped her arms around his back and clung to him. Greer tenderly held her, saying nothing else, and Emery knew he was right. Greer would protect her. Always. That man would've killed her, and Greer had instinctively rescued her. He was her hero.

Had he been Alivia and her boyfriend's hero as well when he'd killed Travis to save their lives? Of course he had. Greer was a hero all the way through. Shooting the Voice in the head had guaranteed the man couldn't react and hurt Emery. Had he shot Travis in the same way to keep Alivia and her boyfriend from harm at her brother's hands? Had her brother been a cold-blooded killer? She couldn't digest that any more than she could believe Greer was one.

She didn't want to think about it. So she cuddled into the only safety she would ever need but might not have after today. And she cried harder.

Chapter Eighteen

Greer held Emery until the police came. She selfishly clung to him, knowing soon she'd have to break away from the perfect cocoon of his strong arms and chest. As the police asked them to separate for questioning, she reluctantly pulled back. It hurt. Greer's blue eyes studied her, asking questions she had no answers to.

The questions from the police went fairly quick as she gave one-word answers in the living room and heard Greer doing the same in the kitchen. The police seemed frustrated, and the similarity of their responses almost made her smile. But she wasn't much for smiling right now.

A rap came at the door. A policeman answered and three people walked in. Two tall men with Greer's blue eyes—Greer's dad and grandfather?—and a gorgeous blonde woman standing between them. They each smiled kindly at Emery. She tried to smile back, but her eyes landed on the blonde woman and immediately it registered who she was. Alivia Delta.

She sucked in a breath and put a hand to her throat. The woman from her dream. The one she'd seen Travis gouge with a knife over and over. Her hand slid to her stomach, and she was certain she'd be sick.

"Emery?" Greer's voice came from the kitchen.

She looked at him and he rushed to her side. He gathered her close, and she was so grateful. She cuddled into him as his family slowly approached.

"You're quick," Greer said to them.

"We followed you last night, at a much slower pace, not ticking off highway patrol from Colorado to Utah."

Greer gave a brief smile at that.

Emery couldn't stop staring at the blonde woman. The woman was looking at her too. Her blue eyes were cautious and concerned.

"I'm Papa Delta," the man who'd spoken said to Emery. "It's very nice to meet you."

Emery had no idea what to say. She was so confused. She shouldn't be clinging to Greer and giving him and his family the wrong idea, but she couldn't help herself. "You too," she said in a small voice.

"Keith Delta," the other man said. "Greer's father."

"Nice to meet you," she mumbled. Thankfully, neither of them tried to shake her hand or remove her from Greer's arms. It was her only sanctuary at the moment.

"Excuse me, sir," one of the policemen said to Papa.

His dad and grandpa exchanged a smile and excused themselves to speak with the police.

Emery looked at the woman. She couldn't hold it in anymore. "Alivia."

Alivia nodded, biting at her lip. "I felt prompted to come. I'm so sorry about your brother."

"Thank you." But she had to know. "Did he try to murder you and your boyfriend?"

Alivia cautiously bobbed her head.

Emery's stomach turned over, and she dug her fingers into Greer's back. Thankfully, he didn't push her away or so much as grunt. He held her patiently and sweetly like she'd known he would. She tried to relax her hands.

"I don't think he wanted to kill us," Alivia said as if trying to convince herself and Emery.

"But he yelled at you 'it's time to die'?" She had to hear it from the source.

"He did, but even when he kidnapped us, he said several times he didn't want to kill a gorgeous blonde." She blushed a little at that. "And at one point, he threatened to kill Klein and I called him on it. He admitted that I was right and he wouldn't outright kill him, but he'd shoot him in the shoulder and leave him behind." She studied Emery. "He wanted the secret, but he didn't try to kill us until we escaped and then had the gunfight at the end. It was like being in battle made him flip out and lose his humanity. If that makes any sense."

It did make sense. She'd seen it after Travis's last deployment. Battle did something to him—hardened him, made him cold. He'd been a great brother to her, but he had changed.

"Sometimes the military life does that to a man," Greer said quietly.

Alivia raised her eyebrows as if shocked Greer had spoken so much.

Emery knew Greer's words were true, and it hit her so hard. Greer had shot Travis to save Alivia's life just like he'd shot the Voice to save Emery's. He'd instinctively reacted both times. How could she be so grateful he'd protected her and protected his cousin, yet so sad and conflicted that he'd killed Travis?

"I'm sorry for your brother's loss," Alivia said again.

"I'm grateful Greer protected you," Emery said back.

Alivia gave her a trembling smile, then turned and walked outside.

Emery released a shaking breath. Her brother had almost murdered that beautiful woman. It was horrific to take in. She clung to Greer.

"You okay?" he asked.

"No." She glanced up into his beautiful blue eyes. "I'm not okay. I'm an unstable, volatile, insecure, doubting, vulnerable, wobbly mess, thank you very much."

He let out a half laugh.

She actually smiled at him, but it fell away quickly. She said a prayer for help and strength and then she managed to unclasp her hands from around Greer's back and step away from him. He let her go. Greer would never force her to do anything. She loved him for that. She loved him for a lot of things. Could she forgive him?

"What do you want from me, Greer?" she asked.

Greer looked her over. "Just you."

She swallowed, and tears stung at the corners of her eyes. She wished she could rush back into his arms, but she needed time to heal. A tear spilled down her cheek, and Greer lifted a hand as if to brush it away, but Emery retreated until she hit the wall. She didn't know if she was afraid of him, distancing herself, angry with him, or simply a mess of confused emotions.

"I can't," she murmured, hating herself.

He studied her, his eyes begging her to give him a chance.

More tears raced down her cheeks. She shook her head. "I can't deal with these emotions," she clarified. "I'm such a mess. You need to leave. Please."

He nodded to her, not saying a word—that was nothing new for him—and headed for her front door. His shoulders were slightly rounded. She'd never seem him look defeated like that.

Her heart twisted painfully with each step Greer took away from her. She'd asked him to, but how could he leave her?

At the door, he paused with his hand on the knob. He looked back at her and then he straightened to his full height and turned to face her. "I'm so sorry I killed Travis. I'll pray morning, noon, and night that you can forgive me for that."

The tears kept coming. Emery tried to blink them away, unable to respond.

"You're everything to me, Emery," he continued, his blue gaze intense and searching. "It's insane how we were brought together. I understand that it's unsettling for you. It is for me too. I had never taken a life before I killed Travis. I hated myself for it and prayed for forgiveness and for you to have peace."

She just stared at him. Hung on his every word.

"Papa had me watch the graveside service, and I thought you were the most angelic beauty I'd ever seen in my life. I asked him how I could help you and he said all I could do was pray. It might be twisted, but I feel like God brought us together. I know He can heal both of us and I'll keep praying you can someday love me like I love you and let me heal, protect, strengthen, and shelter you for the rest of your life."

Emery's eyes widened, and silent tears ran down her face.

"I don't know if you've heard any more of the five-nine, sundress song, but it fits you so well. Part of it goes, 'God made her, so I will make sure he didn't waste an angel on me.'"

She'd heard that line in his truck last night. She'd loved it then. She loved it even more coming from his lips.

"You're my angel, Emery Reeder." Greer licked his lips and kept talking, studying her. "I love you. I adore you. I want to savor you. I want to be there for you." He looked her over and said, "And I love seeing you in a sundress."

Emery let out a strangled sound that might've been a laugh or a cry. She tried to memorize each angle of his face, the way his blue eyes were focused on her, the strength and protectiveness that radiated from his tall, powerful body, all the beautiful words he'd just shared with her.

Then she couldn't take it any longer. She turned and ran through the kitchen and into her bedroom. Then she flung herself on the bed, and she sobbed.

Chapter Nineteen

Greer hated nothing quite so much as he hated driving away from Emery's house. It felt like he was giving up on her. It felt like his heart was being ripped from his chest.

They made it home late that night. His dad had driven most of the way while Greer dozed off and on. When they got home, his mom and aunt had far too much food waiting for him, and all of his family showed up that evening. It was rough. He loved them, but he was too messed up over Emery to converse and be normal with his family. None of them would believe all the tender words he'd said to Emery. Sadly spilling his heart hadn't brought her to him.

When his family finally left, he fell into bed and was asleep almost instantly. The next day, Greer went back to his life. At least, he went through the motions. Nothing was any fun without her. Even his animals seemed depressed. He listened to his five-foot-nine song over and over again.

Two long, dreary weeks passed. His family came by often and he appreciated it more than he could express, but he didn't stray from his property except for Sunday services.

He was depressed, but what did everyone expect? He'd had a fun, talkative, beautiful, perfect angel in his life for nine days, and he'd lost her. How was he supposed to deal with that?

Papa came by one night and told him they'd found an interesting connection. The Voice had been identified as Nelson Palmer, Admiral Seamons's aide or "flag officer" as they were known. That was shocking, but it made sense. The guy must've discovered information somehow from Admiral Seamons about the secret and decided he wanted to have it.

Nelson Palmer was also Flynn Wright's biological father. The story had been pieced together, with some help from Colby Newman in his prison cell. Colby had been more talkative after he heard Nelson was dead. Apparently he, Travis, and Flynn had been hired by some unknown source and paid a million dollars up front with the promise of five more if they found the weapon. Flynn had admitted to Colby that it was his father who had hired them under all the cloak and dagger because he wanted to give Colby a chance to be successful and he wanted to have a relationship with him.

Crazy stuff. Admiral Seamons of course was stunned and denied any connection to Nelson Palmer going after the secret, but Papa would have to keep a close eye on his friend. Maybe everything would settle in their valley for a bit. Greer hoped so. He never wanted to so much as point a gun at anyone for the rest of his life, but he'd do what he had to do to protect his family and the secret.

All he really wanted was his five-nine, brown-eyed, sundress-wearing, synonym-spouting beauty who talked too much and made him laugh to appear.

The sun was gone behind the mountains. Greer rested his forearms on the corral and stared at the lake and the mountains beyond. Chandler had a lacrosse game tonight. Would Bentley come? He hoped so. Bentley's visits weren't consistent, but Greer could sure use some company tonight. He'd gotten far too used to having Emery around. He couldn't stop himself from thinking of the lacrosse game Emery had watched with them. Bentley had pushed her against Greer and he'd held her close throughout the game. They'd shared their first kiss that night. His lips tingled at the memory.

He sensed movement to his right. Straightening, he rested his hand on his .500. A flash of pink came through the trees.

Pink?

His heart slammed against his ribcage. The flashes became solid and suddenly there she was. An angel walking toward him from the forest trail wearing a pink and white floral sundress that revealed her tanned neck, shoulders, and legs. Her long, dark hair curled down her back and her brown eyes sparkled at him.

Greer wanted to run to her, but he doubted his suddenly shaking legs would carry him. He leaned against the corral and just stared at perfection walking his way.

She reached him, gave him a flirtatious smile, and tossed her long hair. "Greer Delta. Are you speechless? That's a first."

He laughed. Then he straightened away from the fence and stared at her in awe. "You look like an angel."

"Oh, so you weren't sure if it was a human or an otherworldly being coming out of the mountains toward you?" She winked. "Papa helped me set it up. I thought about carrying a boombox playing our song, but that might've been a little tacky."

He smiled. His eyes drank in the sight of her.

"So ..." She took a breath and looked more serious. "I've been talking with my pastor, Papa, and the good Lord above."

She'd been talking to Papa?

"And every one of them seems to agree that you're the best man any of us knows."

Greer's stomach flip-flopped.

"I need to backtrack a bit." Pressing her lips together, she admitted, "When you shot the Voice to protect me, I was sick and angry, but I loved you for it. When Alivia told me her side of the story, it hit me hard. Travis changed, and he became capable of murder. I hate that for him, and I'm sorry you had to kill him to protect Alivia and Klein."

"I'm sorry too." Words couldn't express how sorry he was.

"I know you are." She took a deep breath. "The Voice originally gave me a video of Travis saying he loved me and his country. The video cut off but Papa Delta found the entire video in the Voice's computer." She swallowed and tears made her eyes bright. Greer wanted to hold her, but he sensed she needed to get this out. "It was awful to see. Travis said, 'I'm coming to realize nobody really honors or cares about vets. You get some token programs or cuts on insurance and house loans, but that's it. I've found a way to change my future. When I get all the money, I'm going to send you some. But I'll never see you again. I love you. You're the only family I ever had and ever needed. Take care, sis.'"

She wiped at her tears. Was this Greer's moment to hold her? Before he could act on the impulse, she kept talking.

"I hated watching that, but it was the closure I needed. The brother I knew and loved was gone before he died. He let himself get bitter and dark and he changed for the worse. I only pray Jesus can heal him on the other side."

Greer nodded. "I'll pray for that too."

"I know you will." Silence fell for a few moments, and then she looked him over. "You look like you haven't slept in two weeks."

He smiled slightly. "You look absolutely gorgeous."

"I know." She winked, but sobered quickly. "What I really know is I need to forgive you and love you." She stepped in closer. "Because I have been miserable, dejected, glum, wretched, cheerless, melancholy without you."

Oh, how he'd missed her synonyms. He'd missed everything about her.

She cupped his jaw, causing Greer's heart to race out of control, and softly kissed his cheek. "I love you." She kissed his neck. "I adore you." She trailed kisses up close to his mouth. "I want to *savor* you."

Greer grinned, and then he did what he'd been longing to do: he pulled her in close and captured her mouth with his. He kissed her long and thoroughly, reveling in the happiness and warmth that exploded through him. When they parted, he lifted her and swung her around. "I love you, Emery Reeder," he yelled, probably scaring his cattle to death.

She laughed and let him twirl her.

Finally, he lowered her close and tenderly kissed her. "I adore you. I will savor you."

She grinned. "I know you will. Just like someday I'll teach you to savor your food."

He chuckled. Then he sang softly, "Five foot nine, brown eyes in a sundress ... God makes the good stuff."

She laughed, and then she kissed him fiercely. Greer returned it and then some. His angel had come back to him. He prayed she'd talk his ear off, tease him, set him straight, hit him if she needed to, list synonyms, kiss him all the time, and never leave him again.

Love, heavenly intervention, and Emery's sweet forgiveness were all miracles he never thought he'd have. He'd offer prayers of gratitude morning, noon, and night for God sending a brown-eyed angel to rescue his heart.

Excerpt - Devoted

Esther Delta glanced over her shoulder but couldn't see the man who'd been shadowing her. She'd caught glimpses of him throughout the morning as she ran errands with her cousins. He'd been in a corner booth at La Hacienda where she ate lunch with her female cousins. She was certain it was Garret Thomson.

Garret was an attractive, seemingly-innocent dentist that she'd gone on a few dates with in Colorado Springs. He'd been a gentleman, until the end of date number three when he tried to check her teeth for cavities, with his nasty tongue. Gross.

She'd taken a leave of absence from her job as an attorney for the Air Force to help her family protect the Delta secret. When Garret had called to ask her out again last week, she'd told him she wasn't interested in pursuing a relationship. It was partially because of her duty to her family, partially because of the absolutely disgusting goodnight kiss, and partially because she never went on more than three dates with any one man. A policy adopted during Freshman year of college to keep her and any man she dated from a nightmarish experience. Avoiding love, commitments that were easily shattered, and months of debilitating emotional weakness were in everybody's best interest.

Why would Garret appear in Summit Valley, the town near her family's valley, and follow her around Main Street? It was concerning. Was he simply a man who couldn't take no for an answer, she'd dealt with more than a few of those, or was he after the Delta family secret? With the stakes of protecting the secret escalating, the entire family was on high alert and everybody was suspect.

She caught his reflection as she glanced at the exterior window of the ice cream shop and shivered. He was across the street, studiously staring into Summit Valley's only clothing store. He boldly met her gaze in the window. His hazel eyes were far too ... calculating, making her think this wasn't a simple case of a man spurned by a woman he was interested in.

Unfortunately for Garret, Summit Valley was far too small to blend in and stalk somebody. Unfortunately for her, she had to figure out why he was following her, without inadvertently giving away any information about the secret. How to draw him out?

Three men walked out of Blake's Grill, the hometown restaurant where Bailey, her cousin Colt's girlfriend and Shelly, her brother Thor's fiancé were both waitresses. The men all wore khaki short-sleeved button-down shirts with Summit Valley Sheriff's Office logos and black pants with guns in side holsters. The man in the middle had a star sheriff's badge on his shirt, filled out his uniform like a confident, tough sheriff should, and boasted the most handsome face Esther had ever seen.

Sheriff Reed Peterson. An ally of the Delta family and close friend as well. His deep-brown eyes focused in on her and the sidewalk swayed underneath her feet. Esther bit at her lip as her stomach did a flip-flop. Reed was a year younger than her and she'd always thought he was incredibly good-looking and fun to tease with, but they'd never dated. Over the past ten years he'd developed into an impressive, accomplished, tough, and tempting man. Over the past few years he'd asked her out multiple times. She'd always had an excuse, not letting herself say yes and fall in love only to lose him tragically. His career alone was a huge red flag. How appealing he was made it even more dangerous.

She was tempted to turn the other direction, rather than give in to the desire to scream yes if Reed asked her out today. She could share three incredible dates with the charming sheriff and then let him down kindly like she did all the others. The problem was, she didn't know if she'd be capable of walking away from Reed. *Would that be so bad?* A rogue voice in her mind asked. She didn't justify the question with a response. Quite often it was better to ignore the opposing counsel's unreasonable questions.

The three men strode confidently her direction. She knew Reed's deputies by name—Isaac Wells and Cameron Boyce. They'd both grown up in the valley but Isaac was enough younger than her and Cameron enough older that she didn't know them well. She wanted to bask in Reed's gaze as he approached, an enticing smile tilting his lips, but she couldn't forget that Garret was lurking across the street. It hit her that Reed was exactly the man she needed at the moment.

In a very uncharacteristic move, Esther ran at the men, hoping none of them would pull their sidearms. She threw herself against Reed's chest and flung her arms around his neck.

His eyes widened, but luckily his arms automatically wrapped around her. It felt insanely good to be wrapped in this handsome sheriff's arms, but she couldn't let herself get distracted.

"Esther?" His voice was more questioning than romantic, but hopefully Garret couldn't hear him.

"Lover!" she all but screamed.

Reed's brow squiggled and shock covered his features. She didn't dare look at his deputies and see how stunned they were.

She was making quite the scene, but she had to make this look real so Garret would leave her alone, or reveal that he wasn't after her but pursuing the secret. Reed would understand. She'd explain ... in a minute.

She leaned in so close their breath intermingled, "Please play along," she whispered.

His gaze registered concern but he nodded slightly. That was all the permission she needed to press her lips to his.

Reed stiffened against her for half a beat and then he caught up. No, he did much, much more than catch up. He surpassed her every expectation of what a kiss with him might be like. His mouth worked with hers in beautiful synchrony. She'd never felt lips like the good sheriff's before. They were soft and firm at the same time. They were warm and tingly. Like taking a warm bath infused with peppermint oil.

He pulled her in tighter and their bodies molded as one. Reed took the kiss to dizzying heights. Esther forgot why she'd initiated the kiss, their surroundings, and any worries. All that mattered was Sheriff Reed Peterson. No man had kissed her like this. She'd never responded like this to any man's kiss. Not even with Roman. She and Reed could keep kissing until the sun set and she still might not be satiated.

A low whistle tried to penetrate their bubble of kissing ecstasy. A throat cleared. A loud laugh came from much too close.

Reed released her from the kiss, but kept her in the circle of his arms. "You all right?" he murmured against her lips, his husky voice and warm breath making her want to kiss him all over again.

"I am now," she managed, blinking up at him.

He gave her an irresistible grin and her stomach flip-flopped again.

* * *

Find *Devoted* on Amazon.

Also by Cami Checketts

Delta Family Romances

Deceived

Abandoned

Committed

Betrayed

Devoted

Compromised

Endangered

Famous Friends Romances

Loving the Firefighter

Loving the Athlete

Loving the Rancher

Loving the Coach

Loving the Contractor

Loving the Sheriff

Loving the Entertainer

The Hidden Kingdom Romances

Royal Secrets

Royal Security

Royal Doctor

Royal Mistake

Royal Courage

Royal Pilot

Royal Imposter

Royal Baby

Royal Battle

Royal Fake Fiancé

Secret Valley Romance

Sister Pact

Marriage Pact

Christmas Pact

Survive the Romance

Romancing the Treasure

Romancing the Escape

Romancing the Boat

Romancing the Mountain

Romancing the Castle

Romancing the Extreme Adventure

Romancing the Island

Romancing the River

Romancing the Spartan Race

Mystical Lake Resort Romance

Only Her Undercover Spy

Only Her Cowboy

Only Her Best Friend

Only Her Blue-Collar Billionaire

Only Her Injured Stuntman

Only Her Amnesiac Fake Fiancé

Only Her Hockey Legend

Only Her Smokejumper Firefighter

Only Her Christmas Miracle

Jewel Family Romance

Do Marry Your Billionaire Boss

Do Trust Your Special Ops Bodyguard

Do Date Your Handsome Rival

Do Rely on Your Protector

Do Kiss the Superstar

Do Tease the Charming Billionaire

Do Claim the Tempting Athlete

Do Depend on Your Keeper

Strong Family Romance

Don't Date Your Brother's Best Friend

Her Loyal Protector

Don't Fall for a Fugitive

Her Hockey Superstar Fake Fiance

Don't Ditch a Detective

Don't Miss the Moment

Don't Love an Army Ranger

Don't Chase a Player

Don't Abandon the Superstar

Steele Family Romance

Her Dream Date Boss

The Stranded Patriot

The Committed Warrior

Extreme Devotion

Quinn Family Romance

The Devoted Groom

The Conflicted Warrior

The Gentle Patriot

The Tough Warrior

Her Too-Perfect Boss

Her Forbidden Bodyguard

Running Romcom

Running for Love

Taken from Love

Saved by Love

Cami's Collections

Hidden Kingdom Romance Collection

Survive the Romance Collection

Mystical Lake Resort Romance Collection

Billionaire Boss Romance Collection

Jewel Family Collection

The Romance Escape Collection

Cami's Firefighter Collection

Strong Family Romance Collection

Steele Family Collection

Hawk Brothers Collection

Quinn Family Collection

Cami's Georgia Patriots Collection

Cami's Military Collection

Billionaire Beach Romance Collection

Billionaire Bride Pact Collection

Echo Ridge Romance Collection

Texas Titans Romance Collection

Snow Valley Collection

Christmas Romance Collection

Holiday Romance Collection

Extreme Sports Romance Collection

Georgia Patriots Romance

The Loyal Patriot

The Gentle Patriot

The Stranded Patriot

The Pursued Patriot

Jepson Brothers Romance

How to Design Love

How to Switch a Groom

How to Lose a Fiance

Billionaire Boss Romance

Her Dream Date Boss

Her Prince Charming Boss

Hawk Brothers Romance

The Determined Groom

The Stealth Warrior

Her Billionaire Boss Fake Fiance

Risking it All

Navy Seal Romance

The Protective Warrior

The Captivating Warrior

The Stealth Warrior

The Tough Warrior

Texas Titan Romance

The Fearless Groom

The Trustworthy Groom

The Beastly Groom

The Irresistible Groom

The Determined Groom

The Devoted Groom

Billionaire Beach Romance

Caribbean Rescue

Cozumel Escape

Cancun Getaway

Trusting the Billionaire

How to Kiss a Billionaire

Onboard for Love

Shadows in the Curtain

Billionaire Bride Pact Romance

The Resilient One

The Feisty One

The Independent One

The Protective One

The Faithful One

The Daring One

Park City Firefighter Romance

Rescued by Love

Reluctant Rescue

Stone Cold Sparks

Snowed-In for Christmas

Echo Ridge Romance

Christmas Makeover

Last of the Gentlemen

My Best Man's Wedding

Change of Plans

Counterfeit Date

Snow Valley

Full Court Devotion: Christmas in Snow Valley

A Touch of Love: Summer in Snow Valley

Running from the Cowboy: Spring in Snow Valley

Light in Your Eyes: Winter in Snow Valley

Romancing the Singer: Return to Snow Valley

Fighting for Love: Return to Snow Valley

Other Books by Cami

Seeking Mr. Debonair: Jane Austen Pact

Seeking Mr. Dependable: Jane Austen Pact

Saving Sycamore Bay

Oh, Come On, Be Faithful

Protect This

Blog This

Redeem This

The Broken Path

Dead Running

Dying to Run

Fourth of July

Love & Loss

Love & Lies

About the Author

Cami is a part-time author, part-time exercise consultant, part-time housekeeper, full-time wife, and overtime mother of four adorable boys. Sleep and relaxation are fond memories. She's never been happier.

Join Cami's VIP list to find out about special deals, giveaways and new releases and receive a free copy of *Rescued by Love: Park City Firefighter Romance* by clicking here.

cami@camichecketts.com
www.camichecketts.com

Made in United States
Orlando, FL
04 October 2022

22994318R00108